AMERICA'S #1 SERIES FOR MAXIMUM CHILLS!

# #18: Washington Wax Museum

# Johnathan Rand

BOCA RATON PUBLIC LIBRARY
BOCA RATON, FLORIDA

# An AudioCraft Publishing, Inc. book

This book is a work of fiction. Names, places, characters and incidents are used fictitiously, or are products of the author's very active imagination.

Book storage and warehouses provided by Chillermania!©
Indian River, Michigan

Warehouse security provided by:
Lily Munster and Scooby-Boo

No part of this publication may be reproduced in whole or in part, or stored in a retrieval system, or transmitted in any form or by any means, electronic, mechanic, photocopying, recording, or otherwise, without written permission from the publisher. For information regarding permission, write to: AudioCraft Publishing, Inc., PO Box 281, Topinabee Island, MI 49791

American Chillers #18: Washington Wax Museum
ISBN 13-digit: 978-1-893699-76-2

**Librarians/Media Specialists:**
PCIP/MARC records available **free of charge** at
www.americanchillers.com

Cover illustration by Dwayne Harris
Cover layout and design by Sue Harring

Copyright © 2006 AudioCraft Publishing, Inc. All rights reserved.
AMERICAN CHILLERS® , MICHIGAN CHILLERS® and
FREDDIE FERNORTNER, FEARLESS FIRST GRADER® are
registered trademarks of
AudioCraft Publishing, Inc.

Dickinson Press Inc., Grand Rapids, MI USA Job # 3924600 September 2011

# WASHINGTON
# WAX
# MUSEUM

# VISIT CHILLERMANIA!

## WORLD HEADQUARTERS FOR BOOKS BY JOHNATHAN RAND!

Yooperland

Indian River

Alpena

Traverse City

**MICHIGAN**

CHILLERMANIA!

*I-75 Exit 313
then south
1 mile!*

Mt. Pleasant

Bay City

Grand Rapids

Lansing

Detroit

Kalamazoo

Visit the HOME for books by Johnathan Rand! Featuring books, hats, shirts, bookmarks and other cool stuff not available anywhere else in the world! Plus, watch the American Chillers website for news of special events and signings at *CHILLERMANIA!* with author Johnathan Rand! Located in northern lower Michigan, on I-75! Take exit 313 . . . then south 1 mile! For more info, call (231) 238-0338. And be afraid! Be veeeery afraaaaaaiiiid . . . .

# 1

"Rachel . . . can you believe they're going to let us see it first?" David asked me in a whisper.

David Rydell is my next door neighbor, and he sits right behind me in class.

I shook my head. "No," I replied quietly. "It's going to be the coolest school field trip that we've ever been on!"

It was September, and school had just started. I was glad to be back. Oh, I was sorry summer was over, but it was great to see a lot of my friends that I hadn't seen since June, when school let out for summer break.

And what a summer it had been! My brother, Derek, and I visited our grandparents in South Carolina. It's usually a lot of fun, but a really crazy thing happened: we were attacked by gigantic sea creatures! We barely escaped with our lives, and my grandparents' home was completely destroyed.

I'm sure glad *that*'s over with! I mean . . . I like a little adventure, but battling huge beasts from the sea isn't my idea of fun.

However, visiting a wax museum? Now *there* was something I could get into.

My name is Rachel Baker, and I live in Seattle, Washington. My family has lived here forever. I have grandparents that live here, and my great grandparents, too.

And it's a great place to live. There's a lot to see and do in Seattle. Of course, Seattle is known for getting a lot of rain, but it doesn't *always* rain here. In fact, there are a lot more places in America that get more rain than we do. But there's a lot of mist and fog in Seattle, so people think that we get more rain. Not true.

And Seattle is also known for the Space Needle, which is a six hundred twenty foot tall rocket-styled building. It was built in 1962 for the World's Fair.

A lot of people are familiar with Mount St. Helens, too, which is an active volcano. It's only a couple hours' drive from Seattle.

If it sounds like I know a lot about Seattle, you're right. In fact, everyone in our class knows a lot about our city. You see, our school had a knowledge contest. Everyone in our class—the entire school, even—took a test to see how much they knew about our city. It was a lot of fun. The class that had the best test scores won a field trip.

And not just *any* field trip.

A trip to a *real* wax museum!

Well, my class *won!*

But the really cool part was that we would get to visit the wax museum before it was even open to the public! Our school principal had made special arrangements with the arts council to allow us to spend a whole Saturday seeing the wax figures and exploring the museum. Sounds fun, right?

Wrong.

Well, sure . . . it *sounded* fun.

But it wasn't going to be.

And if I thought that being attacked by sea creatures in South Carolina was scary, it was *nothing* compared to what was about to happen at the wax museum.

# 2

I was up early—before six—on that particular Saturday. David was up even earlier, and he came to the door with his backpack, ready to go.

"Come on in," I said. "Mom is making my lunch, and I have to finish my cereal."

David took a seat in the living room. "It seems like I've been waiting for this day forever!" he said.

I sat down at the kitchen table to finish my breakfast. "Me, too," I said. "I can't believe our class won the contest."

"By an inch," David said.

And he was right. Mrs. Tupper, our teacher, said that we scored ninety-seven percent . . . one percent higher than the students in Mr. Birch's class. Talk about close!

"I hope the gift store will be open," I said. "It would be cool to have a souvenir from a wax museum."

"Yeah," David agreed. "Like a little wax Frankenstein. That would be great!"

"Here's your lunch, Rachel," Mom said, placing a brown paper bag on the table. "Don't forget to put it in your backpack."

"Thanks, Mom," I said.

I finished my cereal, then I finished packing my backpack. Actually, there wasn't much that I needed to bring with me. The new wax museum was only on the other side of the city.

But we'd be there all day. Everyone was instructed to bring a lunch . . . and then we were all going out for pizza after the field trip. I also brought an umbrella and ten dollars that I'd saved, just in case the gift store was open.

"Ready?" David asked as he stood up.

"Ready," I replied, putting on my sweatshirt.

"You two have fun," Mom said, and she bent down and gave me a kiss on the cheek.

"We will, Mrs. Baker," David said with a big grin. "Today is going to be a blast! I just *know* it!"

Our school is only a few blocks away, and we walked there together to meet up with the rest of our classmates. From there, we would take a school bus to the museum.

The ride to the museum was boring. Although everyone was excited, it was still really early. Lots of kids slept on the bus.

Not David and me. We sat together and talked about what we might see in the wax museum. I'd never been to one before, but I saw some pictures in a library book. The pictures were wax sculptures—people—and they were really cool looking. Some of them looked so lifelike that I thought they were real.

"I hope we see a wax vampire," David said as the bus hit a bump. "You know . . . like Count Dracula or something."

"Or a werewolf!" I exclaimed. "That would be awesome!"

Finally, we arrived at the wax museum. The bus pulled into a big, open parking lot.

"Gee, this place is empty," David said, looking out the window at the barren lot.

"It's supposed to be," I said. "The wax museum isn't open yet. We'll be the only ones here. Just us and the wax figures."

As the bus stopped, everyone got up. Half the class was still groggy and sleepy.

"Okay everyone," Mrs. Tupper said. "Don't forget to stick together for the tour. Afterwards, you'll be allowed to buddy-up and explore the museum in groups."

"That'll be fun," I said.

"Yeah," David agreed as we shuffled along the aisle with other students, making our way toward the front of the bus. "It'll be a lot of fun exploring on our own."

We got off the bus and walked across the parking lot. It was cold and windy, and the sky was iron-gray. Other students were waking up a little more, and I could feel a tingle of excitement as we got closer and closer to the door.

But I also felt something else:

*Fear.*

I felt a small pang of fear knotting in my belly.

*Why?*

It was only a wax museum, filled with wax figures.

*What was there to be afraid of?*

Plenty . . . as David and I were about to find out.

# 3

Walking into the wax museum was like walking into a big, dark room. The front doors were all glass, and they opened into a lobby. To the right were several ticket windows with 'closed' signs draped in front of them. To the left was a glass-walled gift store. There were no lights on inside the store, but we could see shelves and racks of gift items in the shadows. Like the ticket windows, there was a big 'closed' sign in front. Next to the sign was a wax sculpture of a man wearing old clothing. He wore a tall, black hat. The sculpture looked like he was from the 1800s.

"Rats," David said, pointing to the closed sign. "I was really hoping the gift store would be open."

"Well, we can still take pictures," I said.

"Yeah, that'll be cool," David said.

But there was something else that was strange.

There was nobody else around.

*Nobody.*

The only people there were the twenty-one students in my class, and Mrs. Tupper, who was busy counting heads to make sure that we were all there.

"Eighteen, nineteen, twenty, twenty-one," she finished. "Good. We're all here. Now, I'd like everyone's attention."

My classmates quieted, and we all looked at Mrs. Tupper.

"While we're here, we all need to remember a few things," she instructed. "First of all, the director of the wax museum has been good enough to allow our class, and our class alone, to preview the museum. Do not touch the wax figures or any other displays that you see. Does everyone understand?"

We all nodded and agreed.

"Good. I've promised the director that we'll all be on our best behavior . . . ."

Mrs. Tupper continued with her instructions, but it was hard to pay attention. I guess that I was just so excited to see everything.

And then, while Mrs. Tupper was speaking, something caught my attention out of the corner of my eye.

A movement.

I looked over toward the gift store.

*No,* I thought. *Rachel, you're imagining things.*

" . . . and many of the things you see will surprise you," Mrs. Tupper was saying.

*There!*

Something moved again. I turned and looked toward the gift store.

*The wax figure—the sculpture of the man wearing old clothing—was gone!*

# 4

*"David!"* I whispered as quietly as I could. Mrs. Tupper was still talking, and I didn't want to get into trouble.

David leaned closer, but he kept his eyes forward, watching our teacher. *"What?"* he whispered.

*"That wax figure moved!"* I hissed. *"It was there a minute ago, but now it's gone!"*

*"Quit kidding around,"* he said.

I glanced over my shoulder, just to make sure that I wasn't imagining things.

The wax figure wasn't there.

I turned back to David, and leaned toward him. *"I'm not imagining things,"* I insisted. *"Take a look. That wax figure is gone!"*

"Miss Baker?" Mrs. Tupper said sternly.

*Gulp.*

"Yes, Mrs. Tupper?" I replied sheepishly.

"Is there something you'd like to share with the class?"

"Uh, um . . . I just . . . I—"

Everyone was looking at me now, and I felt silly. My tongue felt like it was all knotted up.

"It's just that . . . well, when we came in here, there was a wax figure standing by the gift store," I said. "And now it's gone."

I turned and pointed, and received the shock of my life.

*The wax figure hadn't moved at all! He was standing in the exact same spot, in the very same position that he had been!*

Something really weird was going on.

"He looks like he's still there to me," Mrs. Tupper said.

Around me, my classmates were rolling their eyes and snickering. Amber Caplin frowned and gave me a nasty look. Amber has never liked me, and I don't know why. I've never done anything to her.

*"Quit goofing around,"* she snapped quietly. *"You're going to get us all in trouble."*

I was going to say something, but I decided not to. I didn't want Mrs. Tupper mad at me.

". . . as I was saying," Mrs. Tupper continued, and while she spoke, I turned slowly and glanced over my shoulder.

The wax man was still there, frozen in place.

*Rachel,* I thought, *you are cracking up.*

I returned my attention to Mrs. Tupper.

". . . and if the day goes well and everyone follows directions, we'll all go out for pizza before returning to the school."

Everyone began to chatter, and Mrs. Tupper raised her hands to silence us. "Remember," she said, "that's *only* if everyone follows directions."

I turned and looked behind me.

The wax figure was still there.

I shook my head, not knowing how I could have imagined such a thing.

*Sheesh,* I thought. *Wax figures can't move on their own.*

"The boys' restroom is over there," Mrs. Tupper said, pointing, "and the girls' is over there. We'll take just a few minutes, and then begin the tour."

The chattering and giggling started again as our class broke up. David wandered off, but I wanted to check something.

I wanted to see the wax man up close.

I walked over and stood near the tall figure. His skin was a little shiny, like plastic. He had black hair and a mustache, which looked very real.

I stepped closer, inspecting the figure's hand. It was the same color as human skin, except it looked glossy.

I reached my hand out, then looked around.

No one was watching. I knew that Mrs. Tupper said not to touch anything, but, maybe, just this once, to satisfy my curiosity . . . .

Slowly, I reached closer. My index finger was almost touching the figure's hand.

I looked around again. Some students were peering through the windows of the gift shop, and a few more were taking turns at the drinking fountain.

I turned my attention again to the ominous figure looming over me. The man was staring past me, gazing into nothing. His eyes were frozen balls of wax.

Cold and lifeless.

My finger touched the back of his hand.

Suddenly the figure sprang to life! His cold hand grasped my wrist, and held on tightly.

And then I was screaming, screaming as loud as I could.

# 5

Everything was a blur as I leapt away, breaking from the man's grasp so quickly that I almost fell over backward. Several of my classmates stopped what they were doing.

"Whoah!" someone exclaimed. "You're a real dude!"

"Right you are," the wax figure said, reaching up and removing his black hat. He took a bow. "I am Mr. Lakley, the museum director."

My classmates began to gather around, marveling at Mr. Lakley.

"You look like you're made out of wax!" David piped.

"Yeah, you fooled all of us," someone said.

"Just a little fun to begin our day," Mr. Lakley said. "I made myself up to look like a wax figure to show you how lifelike the figures are. You'll be amazed when you see them."

"But . . . but you disappeared!" I exclaimed. "You were there one minute, and gone the next!"

"I thought I heard my office phone ringing," Mr. Lakley replied. "I just went around the corner to check, then I returned to this spot."

"Well, you sure freaked me out," I said.

"I didn't mean to scare you," Mr. Lakley said to me. "But I *do* want to remind everyone to please keep your hands away from the wax figures. Many hours of hard work have gone into crafting each and every one, and they are very valuable."

"How valuable?" Amber asked. "Like . . . millions of dollars?"

Mr. Lakley laughed and shook his head. "No," he chuckled, "not quite *that* valuable. But they are very, very expensive. Irreplaceable, in fact."

"What does 'irreplaceable' mean?" one of my classmates asked.

Mrs. Tupper spoke. "It means they can't be replaced," she said. "That is why it is such a privilege for our class to be allowed to tour the museum all by ourselves."

"We'll begin the tour in just a few minutes," Mr. Lakley said. "I'm going to remove this make-up in my office, and I'll be right back."

Mr. Lakley turned and walked off, and the heels of his shoes clack-clacked on the wood floor.

The crowd of students dispersed, and more chattering arose. I got in line at the drinking fountain, and David walked up behind me.

"That was funny," he said, grinning. "I was just walking out of the bathroom when I saw him grab you. You should have seen the look on your face!"

"He really freaked me out," I said. "He looked like a wax figure . . . but then again, he looked so real."

"That's because he *is* real," David replied.

I took a drink from the fountain while David slipped the backpack from his shoulder. "I'm not going to haul this around all day," he said, and he walked across the hall and set his pack down on the floor next to the gift shop, leaning it against the glass window.

That was a good idea. My backpack carried only my lunch and a small umbrella, but I didn't want to have to carry it around everywhere. I slung the pack off my shoulder and dropped it next to David's . . . and that's when I saw it.

*A face.*

Someone moved in the gift shop!

I only saw him for a moment, but it looked like the face of a man. When he saw me looking, he ducked down behind a shelf.

"Did . . . did you see that?" I asked David.

"See what?" he replied, turning toward me. He'd been looking the other way.

"I thought I saw someone in there," I said.

"You're imagining things," David said.

"No, I'm not," I replied, shaking my head. "I didn't imagine the museum director moving, and he turned out to be real."

David and I peered through the glass. All I could make out were dark shadows of shelves and racks.

But there was no movement.

"I guess it was nothing," I admitted. "I'm just jittery."

"How are you, Jittery," David smirked, holding out his hand. "I'm David."

I shook my head and rolled my eyes. David was always joking around like that.

The clack-clacking of shoes could be heard in the distance, coming closer. We turned to see Mr. Lakley approaching. He was wearing a different suit, a newer one, and he looked a lot different than he did a few minutes ago.

"Everyone ready?" he said cheerily.

Cries of "yep!" and "you bet!" could be heard as we gathered around.

"Wonderful!" Mr. Lakley said. "The tour is about to begin."

"This is so cool!" David exclaimed. "This is going to be the tour of a lifetime!"

David was right. It was going to be the tour of a lifetime.

But it would also be a different kind of tour altogether.

Our tour of the wax museum would soon turn into a tour of terror . . . .

When we were all gathered around, Mr. Lakley held up his hand. "As we begin our tour," he said, "make sure to note the unique construction and layout of the building. The wood floor beneath your feet is the same floor that was laid down when the building was constructed over a hundred years ago." Then he pointed to the wall, and then to the ceiling. "You'll notice that the designs and patterns on the walls and ceiling are very intricate."

*"What's 'intricate' mean?"* David whispered in my ear.

*"I think it means really involved and ornate,"* I whispered back.

David thought about this. *"Oh,"* he said quietly. Then: *"What's 'ornate' mean?"*

Amber Caplin heard him, and she turned. *"Shhh!"* she hissed, and then turned away.

Mr. Lakley began walking down the hall, and our group followed. Mrs. Tupper was right behind the museum director, who continued talking about the building.

"The wax museum is laid out in large rooms," he said as he walked. "Each room has been designed with a particular theme in mind. For instance, we have a room with wax sculptures of some of the world's most famous musicians. Another room features great athletes."

There were some excited gasps at this point, mostly from the boys.

"Other rooms include world leaders," Mr. Lakley continued, "movie stars, and even famous monsters from film and books."

This caused a dull roar of gasps and excited chattering.

*"Yes!"* David said. *"I can't wait to see the wax monster room!"*

Mr. Lakley stopped and turned around, facing our group.

"Here we are," he said. "Our first stop. This room features presidents of the United States."

"All of them?!?!" someone gasped.

Mr. Lakley laughed. "No, not all of them," he said. "The room isn't big enough, as you'll see. This way." He pushed open a large oak door and extended his arm, motioning us inside.

We entered the room in a single file. Mr. Lakley was the last one in.

"This is cool!" someone said.

"They look so real!" I heard Amber Caplin say.

And they did, too. The wax figures were mounted on pedestals about a foot off the floor. There was black velvet skirting around each pedestal, and, at the feet of each president, a brass plaque was mounted.

And the walls!

They were painted in different scenes. Murals, they're called. There was a civil war scene, and a painting of the white house. Every wall was painted from the floor to the ceiling. They looked really cool, and I knew that someone had put a lot of time and effort in creating the art work.

From behind us, Mrs. Tupper spoke. "Class, before we walk through this room, let's have a little quiz."

A low groan rumbled through the room.

"I think this will be fun," she said. "Stay right where you are. I'll point to a wax figure, and I'd like someone to tell me who it is."

Actually, the quiz was kind of cool. I recognized most of the presidents, and Mrs. Tupper called on me when she pointed to Franklin D. Roosevelt. Which, of course, I knew from studying him in our history book.

When the quiz was over, Mr. Lakley told us to take a few minutes to look around and inspect the wax sculptures.

"He sure looks real," David said, leaning toward the sculpture of Thomas Jefferson.

"Don't touch him," I warned.

David rolled his eyes. "I won't," he said. "Besides . . . that's your job."

The brass plaque at the sculptures' feet told all about each president, listing interesting facts about his life and accomplishments. Mrs. Tupper told us to pay close attention, as she might give us another quiz on Monday.

We spent fifteen minutes in the president's room before Mr. Lakley told us to line up at the door. He and Mrs. Tupper lead us out into the main hallway. I was the last one out, and the door swung shut behind me.

Suddenly, Mr. Lakley stopped and turned. He looked right at me.

"Miss," he said, "could you please go back into the room and turn off the light?"

"Sure," I said with a shrug. I turned and opened the door.

A thin chill slithered down my spine. It was odd. I mean . . . there was nothing to be afraid of.

I looked around the room, and the presidents seemed to glare back at me with haunting, waxy eyes. That was a little spooky, I guess.

But that wasn't the spookiest part.

*The spookiest part was that I could hear strange whispering—voices—coming from the statues!*

7

I didn't move. I stood in place, motionless and transfixed, trying to understand what I was hearing. The voices were soft and quiet, and I couldn't make out what was being said.

But one thing was certain: the sounds I heard were *voices*. I might not have been able to hear what was being said, but I know human voices when I hear them.

Suddenly, I wanted out of the room as soon as possible. My arm darted out and flicked the light switch on the wall. The room went dark, and I flung the door open and entered the main hallway.

The class had already started to wander farther down the hall, with Mr. Lakley talking. I hurried to catch up with the group.

*What could that have been?* I wondered. *I know what I heard. I heard voices. But voices . . . from where? From whom? The wax presidents?*

Nonsense. The sculptures were made of wax. They weren't real. They couldn't speak.

Could they?

No. Impossible.

*Then . . . just what did I hear?*

When I was little, I remember laying in my bed. It was a warm summer night, and I couldn't sleep. Oh, I was tired, but a friend from across the street had told me a story about a terrible monster that stalked the neighborhood at night.

Well, I was sure I could hear the creature scratching at my house, just beneath my window! He was scratching to get in! I screamed until my mom and dad came running, bursting into the room to see what was the matter. As it turns out, it wasn't a monster at all. It was only a small branch from a shrub that grew close to the house. A breeze was causing it to move and scratch the siding beneath my window!

My point is, usually when you think that something really bad is happening—like monsters attacking—it usually turns out to be something else entirely.

So then . . . where were the voices coming from? Were they actual *human* voices? Maybe I didn't hear voices, but just mice. Could that be it?

I had to know. I just *had* to.

And so, as the rest of my classmates rounded the corner, I hung back to get a drink of water at a nearby fountain. I sipped for a moment, until no one was watching.

Then I turned and ran as quietly as I could, back to the closed door.

Back to the presidential room of the wax museum.

Back to where I heard the voices.

I looked up and down the hall.

There was no one else around.

I reached out, and my hand grasped the metal door handle.

I pulled.

The door opened without a sound . . . but, right away, I knew something was odd.

*The lights were on!*

I was sure I had turned them off! Yet, now, the room was again brightly lit. I paused to listen, but I didn't go into the room.

Nothing.

*How did the lights get turned on?* I wondered. *That just doesn't make any sense. I just turned them off a few moments ago. I know I did.*

But I didn't hear any voices. Maybe I had been imagining things, after all.

Instead of going into the room, I reached my arm around, feeling the wall for the switch . . . and that's when something suddenly snatched my wrist and pulled me into the room!

It happened so fast that I didn't have time to get away. I pulled and tried to jerk back, but the grip on my wrist was too strong. I was just about to scream when I saw who my attacker was:

*David!*

"What are *you* doing here?!?!" I demanded, finally snapping my wrist from his grasp. My voice was trembling, as I was still shaking from the scare.

"I didn't know it was you," David said. "I thought you were someone else."

"Well, you scared me!" I said angrily. "I didn't know it was you. It could have been a hairy monster or something!"

"Yeah, right," David said.

"And what were you doing in here, anyway?" I asked.

"I thought . . . I thought . . . oh, never mind."

"What?" I pressed.

"I thought that I heard voices," David said, looking around the room. "Just as our class was leaving. They were faint, and it was hard to hear over all the talking going on, but I thought I heard someone talking."

"You heard it too?!?!" I exclaimed.

David lit up. "You . . . you mean . . . you—"

I bobbed my head. "When I came back in to turn out the lights, I heard whispering. I didn't see anyone, but I thought I heard voices. That's why I came back here. I wanted to prove to myself that I wasn't going crazy."

"Well, I thought I heard them, too," David said.

"But how did you get in here without being seen?" I asked.

"You didn't see me when you came out of the room because you looked the other way, toward the group. I was actually just a few feet away, but you didn't look in my direction. I was going to get a sip of water from the fountain on the other side of the hall. When you went to join the group, I came back in here."

We stopped talking and looked around the room, listening . . . but there was nothing to hear except our own breathing.

"Well," I said quietly, "whatever, or whoever it was, they're gone now. Come on. We'd better catch up with the class, or we're going to get into trouble."

I opened the door and David flicked off the light. We scurried down the hall, around the corner, then around another, until we saw our class. Thankfully, they were all walking, facing the other way, so no one saw us. We tiptoed with giant steps and made our way to the back of the group. No one knew we had been missing.

Mr. Lakley was talking, and he stopped and turned. "Does anyone have any questions?" he asked.

"How old is this building?" someone asked.

"It's about one hundred years old," Mr. Lakley replied. "Originally, it was built as a warehouse. When the building's owner died years ago, ownership of the warehouse was transferred to the city. It remained closed for years, until it was given to the local arts council. They spent three years making renovations and repairs. However," he continued with a twinkle in his eye, "there were some strange things that happened while it was being fixed up."

47

"Like . . . like what?" Amber Caplin asked.

"Well," Mr. Lakley said, "some of the workers reported seeing and hearing strange things. Things that couldn't be explained. In fact," he said as he looked around at the walls and the ceiling, "some of the workers believe that this building is haunted."

David and I looked at each other in disbelief.

I raised my hand, and Mr. Lakley looked at me.

I stammered as I spoke. "You . . . you mean that there are . . . are—"

"Yes," Mr. Lakley said with a nod. "We might not be the only ones here."

"Who . . . who else might be here?" someone asked quietly.

Mr. Lakley looked around, and very quietly, he said the word that sent a wave of shivers rushing through my entire body.

*"Ghosts,"* he said as he looked around. *"Ghosts."*

*Ghosts.*

Mr. Lakley's voice echoed in my head.

*Ghosts.*

*Is that what we heard in the presidential hall?* I wondered. *Ghosts?*

Again, I looked at David, and his eyes were wide. I could tell he was just as spooked as I was.

The group began to move again, and Mr. Lakley continued telling us about the building, about the wax figures and how they were made. He told us that we'd learn a lot more later in the day when we would see a special hour-long movie in the museum theater about how the wax sculptures were created.

Finally, we arrived back at the lobby.

"Okay, everyone," Mrs. Tupper said, "we're now going to split into groups of three. Mr. Lakley has given us special permission to explore the museum on our own, in small groups."

An excited buzz rose.

"How cool!" someone said.

"However," Mrs. Tupper continued, "we must remember the rules. You may go into any of the rooms, but do not touch any of the sculptures."

Someone raised their hand. "Can we take pictures?"

Mrs. Tupper looked at Mr. Lakley, who nodded. "Yes," he said. "Pictures are fine. Later, we'll open the gift shop. If anyone would like to buy a souvenir, they may do so at that time."

All of this was good news. But the bad news came when we were organized into groups of three. David and I stayed together, and my classmates all gathered into their own trios. However, there was still one person who didn't have a group.

Amber Caplin.

We realized it too late. Mrs. Tupper saw Amber, saw David and me, and spoke.

"Amber," she said, "you join Rachel and David."

*Oh, great,* I thought. *I can't stand her. Now we have to spend the rest of the day with her.*

Amber wasn't all that happy, either. She frowned as she approached.

"Well, this will be a fun day," she said sarcastically.

"Yeah, a real barrel of monkeys," David said. "Matter of fact, I'm looking at a monkey right now."

Amber stuck her tongue out.

"There are clocks in all of the halls," Mrs. Tupper said. "Pay attention to the time, and we'll meet back here in the lobby in forty-five minutes."

The chattering erupted again as groups of students headed out in different directions. Most were headed for the rooms that we hadn't seen on our first tour.

"Let's go see the monster room," Amber said.

"That'll be cool," David said, "but I want to go back to the presidents room, first."

"Yeah, me, too," I said.

Amber looked angry. "Why?" she demanded. "We've already been there."

I looked at David, and he looked at me.

"We . . . just want to," I said to Amber. "When we were there a while ago, we thought we heard voices."

51

"Oh, brother," Amber said, slapping her palm to her forehead.

"Come on," David said. "We'll only be a minute. I want to see the monster room, too. But let's go back to the presidents room first."

We started walking, and Amber reluctantly followed. She was mumbling to herself, saying something about how silly this was.

A group of three students rushed past, nearly running. They vanished around a corner.

Soon, we were at the presidential room. There were no other students around.

"This will just take a minute," I said, and I grabbed the door handle and pulled.

We were greeted by a black wall of darkness. David reached around the wall and flicked the switch, and the lights lit up the room.

"I don't hear a thing," Amber said. "Let's go."

"Hang on a minute," I said. "We haven't even gone inside yet."

David entered first, followed by me, then Amber. We stopped and looked around, listening.

"I don't hear a thing," Amber whined.

"Shhh!" I hissed.

Silence. There were no voices, nothing to hear at all, except some giggling and laughter as some of our classmates passed by in the hall.

Other than that . . . *nothing*.

"Told ya," Amber said. "Can we go now? You guys are wasting my time."

Suddenly, David pointed. "I knew something weird was going on!" he exclaimed. "Look!"

I looked where he was pointing, but I didn't see anything.

"What is it?" Amber replied tiredly. "A ghost?"

"There's nothing there," I said to David.

"That's what I mean, Rachel! Look! That's where the sculpture of George Washington is supposed to be! It was there fifteen minutes ago . . . but now, it's *gone!*"

# 10

Now we had *two* mysteries.

Where had the voices come from?

And—

Where did the wax sculpture of George Washington go?

We were perplexed.

"He was here a few minutes ago," I said, echoing David's words. "He couldn't have just walked away on his own."

"Maybe he melted," Amber snapped.

David and I ignored her, and we started walking through the room, past sculptures of other presidents. When we arrived at the felt-covered pedestal where

George Washington had been, we found nothing . . . except the brass plaque where his feet had once been.

David scratched his head. "This is weird," he said, looking around. "I thought Mr. Lakley said that the statues were heavy."

"He did," I said, nodding my head.

"Somebody probably moved him," Amber said sharply. "Can we go now? I don't want to spend all day hanging around plastic presidents."

"They're not plastic, they're wax," I pointed out.

Amber rolled her eyes and stomped a foot. "Whatever," she said. "Let's just *go,* already."

"In a minute," David said. "Let's walk around and see if any other sculptures are missing."

We walked slowly through the room, turning our heads from side to side, looking for empty pedestals.

And listening, too. Earlier, I had heard voices, I was sure. As I walked, I strained to hear anything that seemed out of the ordinary, but I heard nothing. Except, of course, the sniffling and whining of Amber, who was sluggishly trudging behind us with her arms folded across her chest. She wasn't having fun at all.

"They all look like they're here," I said. "George Washington is the only one that's missing."

"Mystery solved," Amber said. "Old George is gone. Now, let's do the same thing, and get out of here."

David walked back to the pedestal where George Washington should have been. He got down on his hands and knees, peering keenly at the floor.

"What are you looking for?" I asked.

"I don't know," David replied.

"You look silly," Amber snapped. "And you're going to get dirty."

I looked around the room, glancing at the colorful murals, wondering where someone would have taken the sculpture of the president. "Maybe it got damaged," I offered, "and someone came and hauled it away to get fixed."

"Maybe a ghost took it," Amber said.

I shot her a nasty look. I was getting really tired of her, and we'd only been together as a group for a couple of minutes.

David stood and walked across the room. Before he reached the windows, however, he stopped and looked down.

Then he stomped his foot on the floor. It made a hollow, echoing sound.

And that's when we found something that was about to change everything. There was something really strange going on in the wax museum . . . and we were about to stumble upon what it was.

# 11

"Guys!" David said excitedly, "you're not going to believe this!"

Amber put her hands on her hips and shook her head. "I'm *not* a *guy,*" she said adamantly, "and after seeing you crawling around on your hands and knees in a wax museum, I'd believe *anything.*"

I walked over to where David was standing.

"What is it?" I asked.

"I'm not positive," David said, "but it looks like a secret door in the floor."

He stepped back, and I looked down. Sure enough, I could see the outline of what appeared to be a perfectly square hole in the floor. A small, brass latch acted as a lock. What's more, there was even a small hook that was flush with the wood in the door, but when David reached down, he was able to grasp it with his hand.

"It *is* a door!" I said excitedly.

Amber was curious now. She walked to where we stood and peered down at the strange, square door in the floor.

"Well?" she said. "What are you waiting for? Open it."

"I don't know if we should," I said. "We might get into trouble."

"Oh, for goodness sakes," Amber said, and she pushed David out of the way and bent down. Then, she pulled back the latch, grabbed the ring on the floor, and pulled.

The door came up, and beneath it was a series of wooden steps, plunging into darkness!

"Wow!" I exclaimed. "It really *is* a door!"

"I wonder where it goes?" David asked.

Amber slowly lowered the door so that it rested on the floor, fully open. The dark staircase loomed beneath us. There were no lights on, and it made the steps look as if they were being swallowed up by the darkness below.

We listened, but there was nothing to hear. No voices, no movement . . . nothing.

*I wonder if this is where the voices were coming from?* I thought. *After all, they sounded muffled and distant. Maybe there was someone down there, talking.*

"Let's go down and see what's there!" Amber said. Minutes before, she had been begging to leave. Now she wanted to stay, even if it meant doing something she shouldn't be doing.

"That's not a good idea," David said. "I'm sure the museum director wouldn't want us going down there."

"Oh, he won't care," Amber said. "We won't touch anything. Let's just follow the steps to see where they go."

"They probably just go down to a basement," I said.

"Only one way to find out," Amber chirped, and she took a step down. "Are you chickens coming?"

I shook my head. "No," I said. "I'm staying right here."

"Me, too," David said. "I don't think you should go down there."

"You're both a couple of scaredy-cats," Amber said, taking another step.

Then she took another step.

And another.

One more.

Soon, her head was beneath the floor.

"Last chance," she said, looking up at us.

David and I shook our heads. There was no way we were going to follow her down.

Amber took a few more steps, and the darkness engulfed her. We could hear her feet on the stairs, but we could no longer see her.

"Geez, it's dark down here," she said. "I wish I could find a light somewhere."

"Come on back," I called down. "It might be dangerous."

"There's nothing dangerous down here," Amber called back. Her voice sounded hollow and booming. "There's nothing to be worried about at—"

Suddenly, we heard a loud *clunk!* and Amber was screaming, shrieking at the top of her lungs!

# 12

Suddenly, there was another loud thump . . . and Amber stopped screaming.

There were no sounds at all.

We didn't take the time to call out. Amber had fallen, and we knew she was hurt. And, although David and I didn't like Amber, we couldn't just do nothing. After all, she was injured. She needed help . . . fast.

David was first, taking the steps quickly, but being careful not to fall. I followed, and within seconds, we were in darkness. The only light came from the open trap door above.

"Amber!" I called out as my feet drummed the stairs. It was getting darker and darker the further we descended. The air became stale and dry, and carried a faint chemical odor.

"I'm right here!" Amber replied. "I fell!"

"Yeah, we kind of figured," David said, which, for some reason, caused me to laugh.

We slowed, because we were in almost total darkness. There was still a glow coming from the trap door above us, but we had gone down several flights of stairs, and the light was faint and gloomy.

David stopped suddenly, and I bumped into him.

"There you are," I heard him say. "Are you all right?"

"Of course I'm all right!" Amber snapped. "I just tripped on a step."

I peered around David. In the gloom, I could see Amber's dark form on the floor . . . which meant that we had reached the basement, or whatever the place was called. I looked around, but it was too dark to make anything out.

Amber climbed to her feet and brushed herself off.

"You're lucky you weren't hurt," David said.

"I'm fine," Amber replied. "Let's get out of this icky place."

"Yeah," I said. "We're probably not supposed to be here at all."

I turned and took a step up . . . then stopped. David bumped into me, then spoke.

"What's the—"

"Shhhhh!" I whispered. *I heard something!*

The three of us stood on the steps in the hazy dark, listening.

At first, there was nothing to hear except a low hum of what I figured must be the furnace. It was very faint.

But then, I heard something else.

Something that I'd heard earlier.

*Voices.*

Like the sound of the furnace, the voices were faint, like they were a long way away.

I couldn't make out what was being said, but it was definitely *voices*.

Question was . . . *where were the voices coming from? And who was it?*

I thought about what Mr. Lakley said about the strange things that occurred when the building was being renovated. Many of the workers said they saw and heard strange things, and thought the place was haunted.

*But that's just silly make-believe,* I thought. *Ghosts aren't real. They only exist in books and movies.*

*Don't they?*

The voices became louder.

Closer.

*"They're above us!"* David hissed.

Then, I realized that the voices were probably coming from some of our classmates. Or, worse: Mrs. Tupper or Mr. Lakley.

Either way, I knew that we were going to be in a lot of trouble.

I took another step up . . . and stopped.

"You left the door open!" I heard a man say from above. It was a voice I didn't recognize.

"No, I didn't!" another voice said. "I closed it!"

"Well, it's open now!"

"I didn't do it!"

*"Who's that?!?!"* Amber asked, using a louder voice than she should have.

*"Shhhh!"* David whispered.

And from above:

"Well, close the thing, and let's get to work. We don't have much time."

Suddenly, there was a shuffling noise from above, and the squeaking of door hinges.

The light faded.

It grew darker.

Still darker . . . .

And then:

*Slam!*

The door above closed, plunging us into complete darkness!

# 13

Amber started to scream, but she was cut short. In the darkness, David had reached up and cupped his hand over her mouth.

*"Quiet!"* he hissed. *"That's the last thing we want to do!"*

I have to admit . . . I was *scared*. In fact, I was more than just scared. I was *terrified*. It was so dark that I couldn't see a single thing . . . the floor, the steps . . . *nothing*.

Above us, we heard the sound of footsteps fading away.

*"What do we do now?"* I asked quietly. I was so nervous and scared that my voice trembled.

*"We wait for a couple of minutes,"* David said, *"then we go upstairs and get out of here . . . and hope we don't get into trouble."*

So, that's what we did. We waited in silence, in total darkness, listening to the faint motor hum of the furnace.

Finally, after a few minutes ticked past, David spoke.

"I think the coast is clear," he said. "Let's get out of here."

Slowly, we climbed the stairs. It was really weird, trying to walk up the steps without being able to see a single thing. I walked with my arms outstretched, feeling for the walls around me, all the while being careful to raise my feet enough so that I wouldn't trip on the stairs.

Suddenly, my head hit something.

"Ouch!" I said, ducking down.

"End of the line," David said. "Push the door open, Rachel."

I raised my arms up and placed the palms of my hands on the door, then pushed.

The door wouldn't budge.

"It's too heavy," I said. "I can't move it an inch."

David stepped up next to me, and we both tried. Still, the door wouldn't move.

"Amber, help us," David said. Amber did as she was told, squeezing in between David and me.

"On three," I said. "One . . . two . . . three!"

It was no use. Even with the three of us pushing up on the door, it wouldn't budge.

"They must have locked it with the latch," David said. He pounded on the door. "It won't move an inch."

"I want out of here right now!" Amber demanded.

"Hey, you got us into this mess," I scolded. "If you hadn't come down here in the first place, this wouldn't have happened."

"Stop it, you guys," David said. "There has to be another way out of here. We just have to find it. Let's go back downstairs and see if we can find another door."

We descended the steps once again, slowly, cautiously, being careful on the stairs. When we reached the floor, we stopped.

Now, remember: it wasn't just *dark*. It was *completely* dark. There were no lights, no shadows, nothing.

Just . . . *darkness*.

*How are we ever going to find our way around?* I wondered. *I can't even see an inch in front of my face.*

I could hear David moving around. "I found the wall," he said. The next thing I heard were his hands on the wall, making a sweeping sound.

"Rachel . . . try looking on your side. Maybe there's a light switch."

I moved cautiously to the right, waving my hands slowly in front of me until I found the wall.

"What do you want me to do?" Amber said.

"I think you've done enough already," I said.

Just as I spoke, my fingers felt something on the wall. I fumbled with it . . . and suddenly, a blast of light seemed to explode! It was just a single bulb, but because our eyes had become accustomed to the dark, the burst was blinding. The three of us squinted and shielded our eyes.

But when we were able to finally look around and see where we were, we knew that our whole day was about to change.

# 14

We were surrounded by creatures.

At least, that's what they *looked* like. Wax creatures that weren't finished. There must have been a dozen of them. They looked liked incomplete sculptures. They were human in shape, in different poses, but it was impossible to tell who—or *what*—each figure represented.

"Wow," David breathed. "This is so cool!"

Not far away was a big vat. It was the size of a hot tub, and it was filled with a dark, gooey liquid. Above the vat, several loose chains dangled. They were heavy chains, too, and they looked very solid and strong.

"I'll bet that's wax in that vat," I said. "That's where it's melted down."

"But that can't be," Amber said. "Mr. Lakley said that the wax figures weren't made here. They were made somewhere else . . . and shipped to the museum."

Amber was right. I remembered the museum director telling our class that all the wax figures had been made by master artists. Some were even made in other countries!

David was the first to move, and I followed him. He slowly walked up to one of the unfinished wax figures and reached out his hand.

"Hey," Amber said, "you're not supposed to touch. Mr. Lakley said so."

David rolled his eyes and ignored her. Very gently, he touched the arm of the wax sculpture.

"It's wax, all right," he said.

I, too, touched the figure with my finger. The wax felt cool and hard.

David walked over to the vat of liquid. He dipped his finger in, and sniffed it.

"Eww," he said, wiping the finger on the edge of the vat. "Whatever that is, it's *not* wax. It smells like some sort of glue."

"This is getting more and more confusing by the minute," I said. "First, we hear voices. Then, the sculpture of George Washington is missing. Then, we find a hidden door in the floor. Now, we find this."

"How about finding a way out of here?" Amber said impatiently. "If Mrs. Tupper comes looking for us, we're going to be in a lot of trouble."

As much as I didn't want to admit that Amber was right about *anything,* she was right this time. I don't think our teacher or the museum director would be happy to find out that we were in the basement of the museum . . . or whatever this place was called.

"Well, we can't go out the way we came in," I said. "We'll have to find another way out."

Oh, we'd find our way out without too much trouble. However, we were about to discover a few other things—scary things—that led to a whole *lot* of trouble . . . .

# 15

"There's got to be another door, somewhere," David said. "Come on." He started walking, and I followed him. Amber was behind me, and we zig-zagged around the crude wax figures until we'd reached the far side of the basement.

*"There!"* David said, pointing.

Up ahead, there was a short set of steps . . . leading right up to a door!

We hustled up to it. Thankfully, it wasn't locked and opened easily.

Now, we were in a hallway, but it was very short. Another series of stairs wound around to the left, and we wasted no time going up them. There were only a couple of flights, and, at the top, two metal doors—both of them unlocked. David and I pushed them open, emerging onto the main floor of the wax museum.

"We made it," Amber said. "This is the main level."

"Let's find Mrs. Tupper and Mr. Lakley," I said. "We've got to tell them what we've found."

"But what *have* we found?" Amber said. "Other than a basement, and I'm sure Mr. Lakley knows about that."

"We should tell them about the missing statue and the voices," David said. "Mr. Lakley will probably want to know about that. Come on. Let's find them."

We figured Mr. Lakley would probably be in his office, so we checked there, first. The door was closed, and I knocked.

There was no answer.

"He's around here, somewhere," David said. "If not, I'm sure Mrs. Tupper is. Let's search the halls."

But something funny was going on. We went up and down the halls, and into the rooms that had wax figures. I wanted to take some time to look closer at some of the wax sculptures, especially when I poked my head into the room that had the wax monsters, but David said we should wait until we found Mrs. Tupper.

We kept looking, up and down the halls and rooms, and we even checked the restrooms . . . but there was no sign of Mrs. Tupper. In fact, we didn't find anyone at all . . . which was very strange.

"This is boring," Amber said glumly. "I'm not having any fun at all."

We returned to the lobby, and again knocked on Mr. Lakley's office door. Still no answer.

While David and I were knocking, however, Amber tried to open the front door to go outside.

It was locked.

As a matter of fact, as we went around the empty hallways and checked other doors that went outside, we found all of them locked.

Then we began to call out as we walked. Our voices echoed down the empty halls and faded like smoke in a breeze.

And I was getting spooked. The walls and ceiling seemed to close in on us, and I began to wonder if the old building really *was* haunted. After all, we'd seen and heard some pretty strange things.

But even more, I began to realize that we were alone. Our teacher, the museum director, and our classmates were nowhere to be found.

We were trapped—locked in—inside an old wax museum . . . and that's when things really began to get interesting . . . .

# 16

"Where could they be?" David wondered aloud. I looked up at a clock hanging from the wall in the hall.

"Well, we are a little late," I said. "We were supposed to meet back at the lobby ten minutes ago. Let's go back there and wait."

We turned around and made our way back to the lobby. The gift store was still closed, of course, but I peered through the window at the shadows. I had seen something move earlier, and I wondered if I would see it again.

Nope.

I turned away from the glass . . . just in time to see Mrs. Tupper emerge from a closed door at the end of the hall.

"There you are!" she said harshly. "You three were supposed to be here ten minutes ago!"

"We tried," David said, "but we found a trap door."

"We got stuck in the basement!" Amber cried. "They made me go with them, Mrs. Tupper! It was all their fault!"

I have never hit anyone in my life, but right then I felt like giving Amber a good slug in the shoulder. Instead, I bit my tongue.

"We're all eating our lunches in the staff lounge," Mrs. Tupper said. "Then we'll continue our tour in groups. If you hurry, you'll have time to finish your meal and join us."

"But one of the wax figures is missing," David said. "In the presidential room. The sculpture of George Washington is gone!"

"I'm sure you just overlooked it," Mrs. Tupper said.

I shook my head. "No," I replied. "He's gone. We're sure. Come and take a look."

"It'll only take a second," David pleaded. "There's something weird going on, Mrs. Tupper. We just don't know what it is."

"Oh, all right," Mrs. Tupper said. "Show me. But we don't have much time."

"Follow us," I said, and we spun. The four of us walked down the hall and around the corner to where the presidents room was—only to make yet another strange discovery . . . .

# 17

David grasped the door handle and pulled—but the door didn't budge.

"It's . . . it's locked!" he said as he struggled with the door. "It won't move an inch!"

"It was unlocked just a little while ago," I said.

Mrs. Tupper placed her hands on her hips. "Well," she began, "Mr. Lakley probably locked it while we are eating lunch. Speaking of which, you'd better get back and eat yours while we still have time. We're going to continue our tour in groups of three, and then we'll gather in the museum theater to watch a movie."

"Wait," I said, turning to David. "Let's show Mrs. Tupper what we found. You know . . . down in the basement."

"I hope you three haven't been going places you shouldn't be," Mrs. Tupper said sternly.

"It was their fault, Mrs. Tupper," Amber said. "They made me follow them."

I shot her a nasty look, and David did the same.

"Follow them where?" Mrs. Tupper asked.

"Into the basement," David said. "Well, at least, we *think* it's a basement. We found some unfinished wax sculptures and a big tub of glue or something."

"But Mr. Lakley said that the wax statues weren't created here in the museum," Mrs. Tupper said. "And besides . . . you weren't supposed to be there."

David and I nodded. "Well, Amber started it," I said. "She went into the basement. We only went down because we thought something had happened to her. Come and have a look. We can show you."

"I think we've spent enough time," Mrs. Tupper said. "Now, let's get back to the staff lounge, where you three can eat your lunches."

Reluctantly, we followed Mrs. Tupper back down the hall and into the lobby. David and I picked up our backpacks that were on the floor leaning against the gift store window, and Amber picked up a brown paper sack that contained her lunch. Then we followed Mrs. Tupper to a door on the other side of the gift store. The door opened into a smaller hallway, and we followed it until we reached another door. Mrs. Tupper opened it, and we followed her into the staff lounge, where our classmates were busily finishing their lunches and talking among themselves. No one even seemed to notice that we had arrived.

Amber, David, and I sat down at a long lunch table. I took a sandwich and a bag of baby carrots from my backpack.

Oddly, we ate without speaking to one another. Amber soon left and sat with her friends, but David and I remained quiet. I was certain that he was thinking about the same things I was. Like—

*Where did those voices come from in the presidential room? Who had closed the hidden door in the floor, trapping us in the basement? And where had the sculpture of George Washington gone?*

I hadn't a clue.

But Mr. Lakley would. I'm sure he could solve this mystery for us, just as soon as we had a chance to speak with him.

We finished our lunches. Amber reluctantly rejoined us, and we set out once again to explore the wax museum.

And of course, the first place we headed, despite Amber's pleas, was the presidential room.

Which was now *unlocked*.

David shook his head as he pulled the door open. "This is too weird," he said. The light in the room was off, and I flipped the switch as I entered.

I gasped.

David gasped.

Amber said: "What are you gasping about?"

*The wax sculpture of Abraham Lincoln was missing!*

I couldn't believe it . . . but before we had a chance to investigate further, we were distracted.

Someone, somewhere in the museum, was screaming in terror!

# 18

We forgot all about the missing statue and sprang into the hall. The screaming was coming from one of the nearby rooms, and it sounded *horrible*. Whatever was happening, it wasn't good.

David, Amber, and I rounded a corner and ran into the famous musicians room, where we found Haley Beham backed against a colorful wall, her hands covering her eyes. Mackenzie Morris and Shawna Jacobs were backed up to the wall, too. They looked horrified, but they weren't screaming.

"What is it?!?!" I shouted. "What's wrong?!?! Did you see a ghost?!?!"

Haley had stopped screaming, but she was still heaving and gasping for breath.

"Worse," Shawna replied.

"What can be worse than a ghost?" David asked.

"A mouse!" Mackenzie said. "It ran right in front of us!"

"You screamed because of a *mouse?*" Amber snapped.

"Well, we don't like mice," Haley managed to say.

Other students had heard the commotion and had begun arriving, along with Mrs. Tupper. "What's wrong?" she asked, obviously very concerned.

"It was only a mouse," I replied. "They saw a mouse and freaked."

Students snickered, and began walking away.

"Honestly, Haley," Mrs. Tupper said. "You screamed like that because of a little mouse?"

"Well, I . . . I thought . . . I thought he might bite me," Haley said.

Mrs. Tupper smiled, shook her head, and left the room.

I laughed beneath my breath, and David rolled his eyes. *"What a big chicken,"* he whispered.

We took a moment to glance around the room. It was filled with sculptures of world famous musicians, like Beethoven, Mozart, and a number of others that I didn't recognize. And the walls! They were beautiful, painted with scenes of concert halls and performers.

We left, and wandered back to the presidential room to inspect the pedestal where Abraham Lincoln had once stood.

"For the tenth time today," David said, "something really strange is going on."

"And I'm getting tired of it!" Amber suddenly said. "Everyone else is having a good time, wandering around, checking the place out . . . but we're trying to find out where two wax presidents are. I don't care! I want to have some fun!"

"Fine," David said. "Let's go check out some other rooms. Anything to make you stop whining."

"I'm not whining!" Amber insisted, stomping a foot loudly.

"Whatever," I said. "Let's go."

We wandered around from room to room, looking at all of the wax sculptures. The monster room was the coolest, with wax figures of Count Dracula, the Mummy, a werewolf, the Creature from the Black Lagoon, and even a ten-foot Godzilla! We took some pictures and continued on.

Finally, it was time to meet at the theater to see the movie. When we arrived at the doors, a few of our classmates were already there, waiting. They were talking and laughing, and having a good time. Mrs. Tupper arrived, and she opened the theater doors and we filed inside and took our seats.

The theater, like the rest of the museum, was newly-redecorated, but it looked very old. The seat cushions were red velvet, and very soft. I figured that a lot of time and money had gone into the restoration of the old building.

The movie started, but I had a hard time concentrating. I kept wondering where those two statues had disappeared to . . . and why.

And the voices . . .

And the mysterious basement with the unfinished wax figures.

The images on the screen flickered past, but I hardly noticed them. I hoped we wouldn't have a quiz later.

"I'm thirsty," Amber said, and she got up and left.

I leaned over and whispered to David. *Do you think this place might really be haunted?* I asked.

"I don't know," David said. "I mean . . . I've never believed in ghosts. But we sure have seen and heard a lot of strange things today."

A few moments later, Amber dropped into her seat and almost climbed into my lap. She grabbed my arm.

"You aren't going to believe what I just saw and heard!" she hissed. "You just aren't going to believe it!"

# 19

David and I leaned closer, ducking down so no one would see us.

"What?" I asked quietly.

"I saw two men," Amber replied frantically.

"So?" David said.

"So, they were carrying off a wax sculpture! And I heard them talking, too!"

"What were they saying?" I whispered. The movie on the screen seemed to fade away, and I became wholly focused on Amber in the seat next to me. The entire world seemed to be encompassed in just the three of us.

"One of the men said, *'Hurry, before any kids see us!'* and the other man said, *'Don't worry, I'll lock the theater doors!'*"

*"Oh my gosh!"* I whispered. *"Did you tell Mrs. Tupper?!?!"* I turned and glanced over at our teacher, who was on the other side of the theater and a few rows down. She was sitting between two students who are always acting up.

Amber nodded. "I did, but she didn't believe me. She thought that I was making it up!"

"If they're going to lock the theater doors, we've got to get out of here!" David said.

Quietly, we scrambled from our seats and tiptoed up the dark aisle. Behind us, our classmates and Mrs. Tupper were focused on the huge screen, where a man was talking about the history of wax sculpture.

We made it to the door without anyone seeing us. David grasped the handle and pushed. For a moment, I thought it was already too late, that the men had already locked the door . . . but that wasn't the case. The door opened easily, and the three of us slipped outside and into the empty hall.

"Where did you see the two men?" David asked.

Amber pointed. "Down there," she said. "They were coming out of that door over there."

It was at that very moment that the door we were looking at swung open! Someone was coming out!

*"Hide!"* I hissed, and the three of us ducked around a corner. David peered around to see what was going on.

"Do you see anything?" I asked.

David leaned back and whispered in my ear. "There's a man coming out alone," he said. "It's not the museum director."

"What do you think they're doing?" I asked.

David shook his head. "I don't know," he replied, and then he leaned forward, peering around the corner.

"He's coming this way!" David said. "He's going to see us!"

Not far away was a small alcove with a drinking fountain. We ran across the hall and hid against the wall. It wasn't the best hiding place, and if the man came toward us, we would be spotted for sure.

But he didn't. Instead, he pulled out a set of keys. We watched him separate one key from a small bundle of others, then walk up to the theater doors. One by one, he locked the doors, all the while looking around to see if anyone was watching him. Thankfully, we had just enough room around the drinking fountain, and the man didn't see us.

When he was finished locking the doors, he quickly walked away, in the opposite direction.

"He's leaving," David said. "Come on."

"Wait a minute!" Amber whispered. "Where are we going?"

"We're going to follow him to see where he goes," David said.

"We're going to get into trouble," Amber said.

"We're already in trouble," I replied. "That man just locked the theater doors. Our entire class is inside, and they won't be able to get out. We've got to find out what's going on."

Amber shook her head. "Not me," she replied. "I'm staying right here."

"Fine," David said. "That means you'll be alone if someone comes. There will be no one to help you."

David stepped out from behind the water fountain and jogged up to the corner where the hall turned. Slowly, he poked his head around, then he looked back at us and waved us forward. I hurried up to him, and so did Amber. Apparently, she didn't like the thought of being left alone to fend for herself.

Carefully, I looked around the corner. The man was walking quickly, and he was looking nervously from side to side. Then, he vanished around a corner.

"Let's go!" David said. We leapt around the corner, and walked very fast—tiptoeing—down the hall, following the mysterious man to wherever he was going.

So far, the strange things we'd seen and heard made no sense at all. We couldn't figure out what was going on. Odd things were happening, that was for sure.

But we were now on the trail of a man who had locked the theater doors. Our entire class was watching a movie, and no one had any idea they were trapped inside.

Why?

We were about to find out.

# 20

The man vanished down yet another hallway, and we ran faster, making sure that our shoes didn't slap the floor. We certainly didn't want the man to know we were following him!

As we approached the corner, we stopped. I peered around, and saw the man open a door and go inside. Above the door was a sign that read:

MAINTENANCE

"He went into a room," I whispered to Amber and David. "He closed the door, but not all the way."

We whisked around the corner and tiptoed up to the door. We could hear a single voice, speaking quietly. It sounded like the man might be talking into a telephone.

I turned to David and Amber, placing a single finger to my lips. They nodded. Carefully, we pressed close to the door and listened.

"Yes," the man was saying, "it's all taken care of. The whole class is in the theater, watching a movie. They won't be coming out for about an hour, but I've locked the doors, just in case. That will give us plenty of time."

*Plenty of time for what?* I wondered.

There was a long pause, and I figured the man was listening to the other person on the line.

"That's right," the man continued. "Yes. Yes. We'll have plenty of time to get the sculptures into the truck. Then we can get out of here without anyone seeing us."

So that was it! They were stealing the wax figures! Right beneath our noses, there were men that were going to take the valuable sculptures!

I looked at David. His eyes were wide, as he, too, now understood what was going on. Amber's expression was that of shock, too. Now that we knew what was happening, it all made sense.

Well, not *everything* made sense . . . but pieces were starting to come together.

And one thing we knew: the men had to be stopped. Oh, we weren't going to do anything to stop them. We were just three kids.

But the police needed to know. We needed to get to a phone, and fast.

David leaned forward and whispered into my ear. *"The museum director!"* he said. *"He might be in his office! Let's go tell him!"*

And that's when the door before us suddenly swung open . . . and the man appeared. He was scowling, looking at us in surprise.

We were face-to-face with one of the robbers!

expectancy as that of those journalists that do know
what was happening, I will most gladly

"Well and everything of its class…" But since
were meaning to come together…

And 'tis a thing we know we must fulfil, as the
matter? Oh, we know it going to… that unfold the
through it were but it was she…

Sir Beorhtler hoped to know. Morning went to get
Stone and hide…

Nought knows to warrant…
The meaning time he? he said, We never been here
till… he speak not long…

And that's when the door before the without
going upon… and more that forced me, we said
everything forming it as might…

We were but to take with all of the school…

# 21

Sometimes, when you get really scared, the only thing you can do is run . . . so that's what we did! We took off running faster than I'd ever run before, making huge strides as we plunged down the hall. I had no idea where we were going, but we had to get away.

And another thing:

As I ran, I knew that I'd seen the man before. Suddenly, it came to me.

*That's the shadowy face I saw in the gift store!* I thought. *That's him! That's who I saw!*

Behind us, I heard the heavy clomping of hard-soled shoes on the wood floor, and I knew the man was after us. He was slower, however, and we quickly widened the distance between him and us.

We rounded a corner, and David suddenly slowed and grabbed a door. It was the room that contained the wax sculptures of the monsters.

*"Hide!"* David said. *"Duck down behind a sculpture!"*

The lights were off, but a murky, gray light came in through the windows. Sinister wax figures glared at us, and I was glad we weren't in there at night. I mean, they were only wax figures, after all, but they sure looked creepy . . . especially in the low light. In addition, there were creepy murals painted on the walls, but they were difficult to see without the lights on.

I hurried across the room and hid behind the wax sculpture of Frankenstein. Amber hid behind Count Dracula, and David nestled down behind the Mummy—just as the door opened.

I held my breath. I knew the man was standing in the doorway, searching for us.

*What if he finds us?* I wondered with a shudder. *Then what? Everyone is locked in the theater, so no one is around to help us.*

To my relief, the door began to close. I peered around Frankenstein's leg just as the man's shadow vanished. The door closed, and we were alone.

We were safe . . . at least for the time being.

*"He's gone!"* David whispered. *"Let's go and get help!"*

I stood. "Yeah," I agreed, "but where do we go?"

"Wherever that guy isn't going to chase us," Amber said as she stood up.

I looked around the room. In the gloom, without the lights on, the wax creatures looked mean and menacing. I was sure glad they weren't real.

But that's the exact moment that one of them moved. Out of the corner of my eye, a motion caught my attention. David and Amber saw it, too, and we all turned.

*It was a she-vampire . . . and she was coming alive, right before our very eyes!*

# 22

The sight unfolding before us was truly horrifying. The she-vampire wore a silky, black dress. Her skin was pasty-white, and her hair was long and black. Two sharp, white fangs protruded over her bright red lips.

She stepped from the pedestal onto the floor. I screamed and covered my mouth with my hands. David grabbed my hand and started running toward the door.

*"Wait!"* the she-vampire shouted. *"Don't be frightened! I'm not going to hurt you!"*

Now, would *you* believe it if a she-vampire with fangs was telling you that she wasn't going to hurt you?

Neither would I.

David and I reached the door, with Amber right behind us.

*"Please!"* the she-vampire called out again. *"Let me explain! I'm not what you think I am!"*

David didn't open the door. Instead, he turned on the light, then looked at the horrible creature that had spoken to us.

"Don't come any closer!" David said.

"I won't," the she-vampire replied. "But let me explain what's going on." She spread her arms wide. "I'm not a vampire," she continued. "My name is Mrs. Hemmer, and I am part of the local arts council. We are the ones who have been working to bring this wax museum to Seattle."

And with that, she reached up and pulled the fake fangs from her mouth. "See?" she said. "Not real. They're just plastic."

"Why are you dressed like a vampire?" I asked.

"It's a disguise," she explained. "I had to make myself look like this so I could try to find out what was going on."

"We *know* what's going on," David said. "There are some men that are stealing the wax statues."

"That's right," Mrs. Hemmer replied. "I've known for a week that something was going on, and I suspected that something like this might be happening."

"It is," I said. "We heard the man say that they are going to begin loading wax sculptures into a truck."

"He was talking on a phone," David continued.

"Why are they stealing the wax figures?" Amber asked.

"Well, they're very valuable," Mrs. Hemmer replied. "My guess is that they'll try and get them out of the country and sell them to unsuspecting collectors who don't know that they're stolen."

"What about the basement?" I asked. "We found a door that leads into a basement."

"Yeah," David said. "There are a bunch of unfinished wax figures there."

"Yes," Mrs. Hemmer said, "those wax sculptures are for a class. You see, we're going to hold wax carving classes here at the museum. Students will be using those unfinished figures as their assignments."

"But what about the big tub of gooey glue, or whatever it is?" David asked.

"That's actually a resin being used by the instructor," Mrs. Hemmer said. "It has nothing to do with the wax sculptures. He's using it for one of his other art projects."

Now things were beginning to come together. The voices we'd heard earlier were probably the robbers.

"How many robbers are there?" David asked.

Mrs. Hemmer shook her head, and her shiny, black hair fell over her shoulders. "I don't know," she said, "but I don't think there are very many. The important thing now is to find that truck, and call the police."

"I don't think we should be hunting for any truck," I said. "Our teacher would get pretty mad at us."

"That's right," Mrs. Hemmer said. "That's why I'm going to do it myself."

"Mrs. Tupper can't get mad at us," Amber said. "She and the class are locked in the theater."

Mrs. Hemmer drew a deep breath. She looked shocked. "It's not safe for them to be locked in there," she said. "We have to get them out."

"Why don't *we* try and find a way out for them," I suggested to Mrs. Hemmer, "and *you* go find the truck?"

"Good idea," Mrs. Hemmer said.

"Is there another way to get into the theater?" David asked.

Mrs. Hemmer frowned for a moment, deep in thought. Then, her eyes lit up. "Yes!" she exclaimed. "Yes, there is! There is a door in the back. You have to go through a utility room, but the door is easy enough to find. It's used by the maintenance staff, and there's no lock on it."

"Perfect!" I said. "We can bring our class out that way."

"You've got to be careful," Mrs. Hemmer said. "The men might be dangerous. If you see any of them, stay away."

"Oh, you can bet on that," Amber said. "I'm going to stay far away from those creepy guys."

Mrs. Hemmer walked to the door and slowly pushed it open. I had to admit, as a she-vampire, she sure looked convincing. Very scary and spooky. I was glad she wasn't a real she-vampire!

"All clear," she said. "I'll go look for their truck and call the police. You guys go and get your class out of the theater."

And with that, she whisked out the door and vanished. The door closed, and the three of us were alone.

"Let's go," David said.

We went to the door. I pushed it open slowly, and David peered out.

"Mrs. Hemmer just went into the presidents room," he said. "There's no one else around. Come on."

We slipped out silently, hoping we could make it down the hall and to the theater without being seen by anyone.

Our hopes were dashed in the next moment.

A man suddenly appeared at the end of the hall in front of us!

We turned . . . but there was another man at the other end of the hall, too!

Both of them saw us at the same time.

"Hey, you pesky kids!" one of them yelled. "Hold it right there!"

The two men started running toward us! We were trapped!

# 23

"*Quick!*" I shouted. "*Back into the monster room!*"

The three of us spun on our heels and darted back into the room. I pulled the door closed and twisted the bolt lock . . . just as the two men reached the door. Once they realized they were locked out, they started pounding.

"*You can't go anywhere!*" one of them said. "*Open up this door right now!*"

Like, we were going to do *that!*

"Go get the key from the office," we heard one man order. "Hurry!"

We heard footsteps racing down the hall, fading away. One of the men was gone . . . but I was certain that the other one was standing in the hall, probably just inches from the door.

And it wouldn't be long before the door was unlocked . . . and then, it would be all over for us.

David pointed to the window, and I instantly knew what he was thinking.

*If we can get the window open, maybe we can escape!*

We raced across the room. David reached for the window, found a latch, and threw it open—

But there was one *big* problem.

The window opened up to an alley . . . *two stories below!* If we jumped, we'd break our legs!

"Oh, man, oh, man, oh, man!" David said. "What are we going to do?!?!"

Sometimes, when you're really scared, your brain seems to be running at super-speed. Things just seem to fly through your mind when you need a solution—and that's what was happening to me. I knew that we had to think of something . . . but nothing that I thought of was going to work. Still, I knew there simply *had* to be a way out of this predicament—we just had to *find* it.

I heard keys jingling on the other side of the door, and I knew that time was running out. We couldn't jump out the window, and there was no other exit. Our situation seemed hopeless, and my heart was sinking by the second.

I looked at the open window.

Then, I looked at the door on the other side of the room.

I looked at the window again.

Then, I looked at some of the creatures on their pedestals. They seemed even creepier in the low light.

And suddenly, an idea came to me like a flash of lightning. An idea that was crazy . . . but it was so crazy that it just might work!

and those second thoughts ... and ... heart was not by the
thousand ...

I look that one with me ...

Then, I looked at the door on the right side of this
room.

I looked at the window again ...

Then, I looked at some of the churches, for their
buildings. They looked even more in the low light.

And suddenly, an idea came to me like a flash of
light ... ... but it was too
easy that night might work.

# 24

*"Come on!"* I shouted very loudly. I wanted to make sure that the men on the other side of the door heard me. *"Let's jump out the window!"*

David and Amber looked at me like I'd lost my mind, but before they had a chance to protest, I silenced them by placing a finger to my lips. *"Do what I do,"* I whispered. And with that, I dropped to my knees, lifted the black skirting around one of the pedestals, and wiggled beneath it. I was cramped, but there was just barely enough room for me to fit if I remained curled up in a ball, laying on my side on the floor.

I heard soft shuffling and scuffling, and I knew that David and Amber were doing the same.

But I also heard the jingling of keys . . . and finally, the sound of a lock being turned.

Suddenly, the door burst open. I closed my eyes and hoped they'd heard me shout that we were going to jump out the window. I hoped they would see the open window, and see that we were gone. Then, they might leave . . . without knowing that we were hidden beneath the wax sculpture pedestals.

There was a sudden rush of footsteps, and then they stopped abruptly.

"Where did they go?" a man said.

"Look!" said another. "The window is open!"

I heard more shuffling of feet. They ran right past me! They were only inches from my hiding place!

"They must have got out through the window!" one of the men growled.

"How?" snapped the other. "We're two stories up from the alley!"

"Well, they must've done it, somehow," the other said. "Let's go. We're going to have to hurry, now. Those kids probably know too much already!"

Footsteps ran past me again, and I closed my eyes tightly. I didn't open them until the men were gone, and I'd heard the door close. Then, I pushed the black skirting away and, after eyeballing the room, I slowly wiggled out from beneath the pedestal.

*"David!"* I whispered. *"Amber! They're gone! You can come out now!"*

I heard a noise from beneath a nearby pedestal, and David emerged. Next to him, beneath the wax sculpture of Count Dracula, Amber wriggled out on her belly and got to her feet.

"That was quick thinking!" David said. "We fooled them good!"

"My shirt is all dusty!" Amber complained, brushing herself off. "I've been attacked by dust bunnies!"

I rolled my eyes and shook my head. We'd just barely escaped the robbers, and she was worried about a little dust on her clothing!

"Now's our chance," I said. "Let's get everyone out of the theater and wait for the police to get here!"

We sprang from the room and down the hall, only to see Mr. Lakley walking toward us! What a stroke of luck!

The three of us began explaining things at the same time, until he finally placed his hands in the air, displaying his palms.

"Hey, hey, one at a time," he said. "I can't understand what you're saying. Now . . . what's this about 'robbers'?"

"They've locked our class in the theater," I explained. "The robbers are stealing wax figures!"

Mr. Lakley looked alarmed. "Let's go to my office," he said, "and you can tell me all about it."

I breathed a sigh of relief as we walked quickly down the hall toward the lobby and to Mr. Lakley's office. Thankfully, we'd found him in time. Our ordeal would soon be over—or, that's what I thought at the moment. David, Amber, and I were about to find out that our ordeal was just *beginning*.

# 25

"Now . . . what's all this about 'robbers'?" Mr. Lakley asked. We were in his office, standing in front of his desk. He'd sat down and was glancing back and forth at each of us.

"That's right!" David said. "They've locked our class in the theater, while they load up their truck with the wax figures!"

"Mrs. Hemmer knows all about it, too!" I said.

Mr. Lakley looked surprised. "Mrs. Hemmer? From the arts council? What's she doing here?"

"We met her a little while ago!" I replied. "She told us that she suspected over a week ago that robbers might be plotting to steal the wax sculptures. She's looking for the truck right now, and she's going to call the police!"

"What did these men look like?" Mr. Lakley asked.

"We didn't get a very good look," David said.

"But they were probably ugly," Amber chimed in. "All robbers are ugly, I think."

"How many of them are there?" Mr. Lakley asked.

We shook our heads. "Two, at least," David said. "Maybe more."

"This is a serious matter," Mr. Lakley said. "I'm glad you three are okay."

"But our class is locked in the theater," I said. "They can't get out. We were going to go find a utility room that Mrs. Hemmer told us about. She says there's a door that goes into the theater."

"They'll be all right," Mr. Lakley said. "I have a key to unlock the theater doors. While they're inside the theater, they'll be out of danger."

He had a point. Even though no one in our class would be able to get out, they wouldn't run into any of the robbers.

"What are you going to do?" David asked.

"I'm going to call the police, that's what I'm going to do," Mr. Lakley replied, very matter-of-factly. He picked up the telephone. "This is a job for them to handle. You three wait in the lobby, and if you see anyone, let me know right away."

Mr. Lakley began dialing the number, and the three of us left his office and went into the lobby.

But I was puzzled.

*Why would Mr. Lakley send us into the lobby? Wouldn't he be worried about the robbers finding us?*

"Something's going on," I said to David and Amber.

"Of course, something is going on," Amber said. "But Mr. Lakley's calling the police."

I turned and peered toward Mr. Lakley's office. The door wasn't closed all the way.

"Wait here," I said, and I tiptoed back to the office and pressed myself flat against the wall, next to the door, listening . . . .

"Yeah," I heard Mr. Lakley saying quietly. "What's taking you so long? These three kids know everything!"

I placed my hand over my mouth to silence a gasp.

"Don't worry," Mr. Lakley said. "You just get everything loaded into the truck. I'll take care of these nosy kids. They won't be bothering us anymore!"

*Uh-ho!*

# 26

I tiptoed, taking giant strides, back to where David and Amber were standing.

"Mr. Lakley's in on the whole thing!" I exclaimed. "He didn't call the police . . . he called someone else! He must have called the robbers on a cell phone! He told them that we knew about the plan!"

Amber's eyes grew wide. "We've got to get out of here, somehow!" she said.

"Let's get our class out of the theater," David said. "We'll find the utility room that she told us about. If we can get into the theater, Mrs. Tupper will know what to do!"

That sounded like our best plan. Actually, there wasn't much else we could do. The doors to the wax museum were locked tight, so we couldn't leave. And if we hung around too long, we risked being discovered by the robbers . . . not to mention Mr. Lakley. We had to hurry before he got off the phone.

We ran down the hall, turned a corner, and rushed to the theater doors.

"Wait!" I exclaimed. "Maybe we can get someone's attention by pounding on the doors!"

Amber and I banged on the theater doors with our fists, while David checked to see if, by chance, they were unlocked, which, of course, they weren't.

But no one came to the doors, either. We could hear the movie playing, and it was probably so loud that no one could hear our pounding.

"It's no use!" David said. "Let's find that utility room!"

We took off running again. The hall continued past the theater doors, and around a corner. We sprinted, looking for a door to the utility room.

"There!" David said, pointing to a closed door. It was brown with a gold doorknob. In the middle of the door was a small, brass sign. It had engraved letters that read:

## UTILITY ROOM
## AUTHORIZED PERSONNEL ONLY

"This is it!" I exclaimed, grabbing the knob. I turned it, expecting it to be locked, but it wasn't. I threw the door open and was about to enter, but when I saw what was on the floor, I froze in my tracks.

Then I screamed.

On the floor of the utility room, lying face-down, was a human body!

# 27

Amber screamed. Even *David* screamed, and I'd never heard him scream before. The three of us stood there in shock, staring at the body on the floor of the utility room . . . until I noticed something.

The hair on the body's head didn't look real. In fact, it looked like—

*Wax.*

"Wait a minute," I said, calming down. "That's not a real body . . . it's only a wax sculpture!"

I knelt down and touched the body's arm. Sure enough, it was made out of wax. And it wasn't even a very good sculpture, at that. It looked like one of the unfinished sculptures that we'd found in the basement.

"How did this thing get here?" David wondered aloud.

"I don't know," I said, "but it sure freaked me out."

"I knew it was made of wax all along," Amber said. "I just screamed because you were screaming."

I ignored her. Actually, I was getting pretty good at not paying much attention to anything she said.

"Close the door, Amber," I ordered. "We don't want the robbers to know we're in here."

Amber turned around and pulled the door closed.

The utility room was cluttered with all kinds of things: mops, brooms, garbage cans, a few stools, cleaning supplies, rags, towels, sponges, cans of disinfectants, paint, and boxes. There was so much clutter that it was impossible to see the walls, or the door Mrs. Hemmer had told us about.

"I'll bet it's over there," David said, pointing to the far wall. "Behind all of those shelves with all of that junk."

We got to work moving the items out of our way. After we'd moved a few things, I spotted the door.

"There it is," I said. "Just like Mrs. Hemmer said."

"Good," David said, as he moved a mop and a bucket. "Now, we're getting somewhere."

But it wasn't long before we received more bad news. As we pulled the items away from the door, we found a shiny silver padlock.

"It's locked!" David said. "And that looks like a new lock."

"The robbers probably put it there," I said. "They *really* wanted to make sure our class couldn't get out while they stole the wax sculptures."

"I'm getting pretty tired of this," Amber said. "I want to go home." She folded her arms.

"So do I," I replied. "But we've got bigger problems, right now."

"The only thing we can do now is call the police ourselves," David said.

"But Mrs. Hemmer said she was going to call them," Amber said.

"We don't know if she did or not," David replied. "She said she was going to look for the truck, and then call the police. If something happened to her, she might not have been able to call. They might not know what's going on."

"Problem is, where are we going to find a phone?" I asked. "The only place I saw one was in Mr. Lakley's office."

"That's the one we'll have to use, then," David said.

"But what about Mr. Lakley?" I said. "By now, he's discovered that we took off. He's probably looking for us right now."

"We'll have to be careful, that's all," David said. "If he's looking for us, that means he's not in his office. If he's not in his office, we can use the phone to call the police."

And that's when we heard footsteps approach in the hall. They stopped . . . and the utility room door was thrown open!

# 28

We jumped away from the door, not sure what Mr. Lakley would do.

But it wasn't Mr. Lakley . . . it was Mrs. Hemmer! She still looked like a she-vampire, but it sure was a relief to see her and not Mr. Lakley or one of the robbers!

"Wow!" I exclaimed with relief. "I'm sure glad it's you!"

"Are you all right?" Mrs. Hemmer asked.

"Yeah," I replied, pointing at the closed door that led to the back of the theater. "But this door is locked, too. There's no way for us to get into the theater."

Mrs. Hemmer saw the figure lying face down on the floor, and she looked startled.

"Don't worry," I said. "It's only wax. We thought it was real, at first, but it's not."

"Did you call the police?" David asked. "And did you find the truck?"

Mrs. Hemmer shook her head. "I found their truck, but I wasn't able to call the police. I tried with my cell phone, but it didn't work. The signal keeps cutting in and out."

"There's a phone in Mr. Lakley's office," I said. "We heard Mr. Lakley talking on it."

"That's the one we will have to use," Mrs. Hemmer said, "if, of course, we can do it without the robbers knowing about it."

"But what about our class?" Amber asked. "They're still in the theater."

Mrs. Hemmer looked at her watch. "There's a good chance that they don't know they're locked in," she said, "but the documentary is half over. We've got to figure out a way to get those doors unlocked. There are keys in Mr. Lakley's office. You three stay here, and keep out of sight. I'll go. Keep the door closed. Stay quiet, and you'll be safe."

"But what about you?" I asked. "What if the robbers find you?"

"I'll be all right," Mrs. Hemmer assured us. "You guys just stay here. You'll know when it's safe to come out."

She closed the door, and the three of us—and the wax sculpture, of course—were alone in the cluttered utility room.

"Well, at least the worst of it is over," Amber said. "All we have to do is wait for the police to show up."

We waited in silence for a few minutes. I felt safer, now that we were out of sight, hidden in the room. I was sure that Mrs. Hemmer would call the police, and they would be coming soon.

And it wasn't very long before we heard a commotion in the hall.

Noises.

Footsteps.

Voices.

There was a lot of scuffling and shuffling going on . . . but it wasn't the police, as we were about to find out.

*"I'll get some rope,"* a voice growled. *"I think there's some in the utility room!"*

That's where we were hiding! In seconds, we would be found out!

# 29

We heard the footsteps approach . . . and stop right in front of the utility room door.

The door knob jiggled, and we prepared for the worst.

*"Never mind,"* another man called out. *"We don't need it. Let's just get those sculptures on the truck and get out of here!"*

We heard footsteps again, but this time they were going away. I couldn't believe how close we'd come to being discovered!

*"They're getting away!"* David whispered.

*"Fine,"* I said. *"As long as they don't come back, I don't care. Let the police catch them!"*

After a few moments, all sounds ceased, except for the faint droning of the documentary that was still playing inside the theater. It was really odd to think that our entire class, including Mrs. Tupper, had no idea what was going on around them while they were watching the film!

"Do you think it's safe to leave?" I asked David.

"No way," Amber replied, shaking her head. "I'm staying put until the police come."

"I didn't ask you," I said to her.

David spoke. "I don't know," he said. "Maybe we should wait for the police."

"But what if Mrs. Hemmer wasn't able to call them?" I said. "What if the robbers caught her and locked her in a room or something? Then, all of us are trapped. The robbers will get away."

David thought about it for a moment.

"You're right," he finally said. "Maybe we should go and find out what's going on."

"Not me," Amber said. "I'm staying right here in this room."

"Fine," I replied. I was relieved. I had long grown tired of Amber and her whining, and I was glad she wouldn't be tagging along with us.

"Just don't go anywhere else," David said. "Stay right here in the utility room."

"Are you kidding?" Amber spat. "I'm not going *anywhere*. Not until the police get here."

David moved toward the door. He pushed it slowly, and peered out into the hall. Then he pushed it farther and stuck his whole head out, looking in the other direction.

*"All clear, Rachel,"* he said, waving me toward him. *"Come on."*

I followed him into the hall, and closed the utility room door.

"Where to?" I asked.

"Let's go back to the lobby," David said. "If no one is around, maybe we can sneak into Mr. Lakley's office and use the phone. Maybe Mrs. Hemmer will be there."

We ran softly, silently, our sneakers whispering on the wood floor. As we made our way down the hall, I glanced up at one of the clocks. Our class had been in the movie theater for nearly forty minutes. Soon, the film would be over . . . but the doors of the theater would still be locked.

But at least our class was safe—as long as they remained in the theater.

For us, however, the situation was different. We had no idea where the robbers were, or if they were still around.

In a moment, I had my answer. As we approached the lobby, Mr. Lakley's office door burst open!

# 30

When Mr. Lakley's door opened, it caught us by surprise. However, we were right by the door to the presidential room. David grabbed the handle, pulled the door open, and we darted inside before we could be seen.

*"Maybe it was Mrs. Hemmer,"* I whispered.

*"Yeah,"* David agreed, *"but we can't take that chance."*

I looked around the room and noticed that even more wax sculptures were missing. The robbers had been busy, that's for sure. I just hoped they didn't get away.

David pressed his ear to the door, listening.

"Someone just walked by," he said after a moment. "But I think they're gone . . . whoever it was."

David pushed the door open slowly.

*"There's no one around!"* he whispered. *"Let's use the phone in Mr. Lakley's office!"*

He pushed the door open, and we hustled down the hall, past the lobby and the darkened gift shop, to Mr. Lakley's office door. It was open, and there were no lights on in his office.

We slipped inside, and David pulled the door closed, leaving it open only a tiny bit so we could see out into the hall. I reached for the light switch, but David stopped me.

*"No,"* he whispered. *"Leave the light off. We don't want to let anyone know that we're here."*

The telephone was on a desk. David picked up the receiver and put it to his ear. Then he tapped a few buttons on the phone, but I could tell he wasn't dialing a number.

"What's wrong?" I asked.

"The phone isn't working," he said in despair. "They must have cut the lines or something."

That wasn't good news. If the phones didn't work, we had no way to call for help.

One thing we did find, however, was a set of keys on Mr. Lakley's desk. There were nine or ten keys in the bundle, but we were sure that one of them must unlock the theater doors.

"Now what?" I asked.

David thought for a moment. "Well," he said, "we should probably wait here for help to arrive. If we keep going out into the hall, we're just asking for trouble. If the robbers are still around, they might see us."

"But where is Mrs. Hemmer?" I wondered aloud. "I hope she's all right."

"I'm sure she is," David said. "I just hope she was able to call the police."

The sound of footsteps in the hall drew our attention, and we peered through the tiny crack where the door was open. At the end of the hall, two men were quickly walking toward us . . . and they weren't policemen!

After a moment, I recognized Mr. Lakley. I figured the other guy was probably one of the robbers. They were walking quickly, taking long strides.

"We're almost ready to go," the unknown man was saying. "All we've got to do is get those last couple of sculptures on the truck."

"Good," Mr. Lakley replied. "We're behind schedule as it is. Let's get out of here. I've just got to get my keys from the office."

I looked at the bundle of keys in my hand.

Gulp!

# 31

We couldn't possibly run, because Mr. Lakley and the other robber would have spotted us for sure. Instead, I gently placed the mass of keys on the desk, right where I had picked them up. Then David and I slipped around the desk, crouched down, and scrambled beneath it . . . just as the door opened and the light came on!

From our hiding place, we could see a shadow darken the floor. There was some shuffling on the desk, and the keys jangled as Mr. Lakley picked them up. Then, the light turned off and the door closed.

*"Man,"* David breathed. *"We've been really lucky. But pretty soon, our luck is going to run out."*

*"Now he's got the keys,"* I whispered. *"We won't be able to unlock the theater doors."*

*"Yeah, but everyone is safe,"* David replied quietly.

Suddenly, the door burst open, and we heard Mr. Lakley's angry voice, and a scuffling of feet.

"And you can just stay in here," he said. "You've caused us enough trouble already."

There was some more shuffling, and the door slammed closed. Then I heard keys jingling, and a loud *thunk!* as the lock was engaged.

*Someone had been pushed into the office! There was someone standing near the desk, only a couple of feet away from us!*

While I was almost certain who it was, I still wasn't sure . . . so I slowly lowered my head until I could peer out from beneath the desk. I saw a pair of black women's shoes . . . and the bottom of a black dress.

*Mrs. Hemmer! I was right!*

David and I scrambled out from beneath the desk and stood, scaring Mrs. Hemmer so badly that she screamed. When she realized it was us, she heaved a sigh of relief.

"How did you guys get in here?!?!" she asked.

"We came in to call the police," I explained, "but the phone doesn't work anymore."

"Yeah," David continued. "While we were here, we heard Mr. Lakley coming . . . so we ducked down beneath the desk. He came in and took his keys, and left."

"That's when he found me," Mrs. Hemmer said. "I came here first to use the phone, but it didn't work. So I snuck into the basement. That's where they found me. I tried to call to the police with my cell phone, but I lost the signal and got cut off. I dropped the phone when one of the men grabbed me and brought me up here."

"Our class is still locked in the theater," David said, "and now, we're locked in here for good."

While David was talking, I had been looking down at the wall and the floor . . . and that's when I saw something.

"Wait a minute!" I exclaimed. "I think we can get out of here!"

# 32

What I saw was an air vent. It was square, and it wasn't very big . . . but I could see through it to the hallway. It was only as deep as the wall was thick. If we could remove the vent grill, I might be able to wiggle through it. David might be able to, as well, but the vent looked too small for Mrs. Hemmer to get through.

"All we have to do is remove the vent cover," I said. "There's another one attached to the other wall in the hall, but we could probably just push it out."

"But then what will we do?" David asked.

"I know," Mrs. Hemmer said. "After you two get out of here, go back down to the lower level, where the unfinished wax sculptures are. There is a service door that goes into the alley. You'll be able to get out and go for help. Just stay away from Mr. Lakley and those men."

"But what will *you* do?" I asked.

"There's nothing I can do until the police arrive," Mrs. Hemmer said, shaking her head. "They'll be able to get me out of here. The important thing is for you two to get out of here and contact the police."

There was a clock on the wall. In ten minutes, the movie playing in the theater would be ending. That would mean that our class would be leaving the theater . . . or, trying to, at least. With the theater doors still locked, they wouldn't be able to get out. I just hoped that no one would panic.

The vent cover was easy enough to pry off. Then, David sat down and used his foot to push the other cover. It came off with a single, hard kick, and clattered to the floor in the hall.

"I'll go first," David said, and he pushed both feet through the vent. Clearly, it wasn't going to be easy. The space was smaller than I'd thought, and when David was at his waist, it became a struggle.

"Push me through," he said, and Mrs. Hemmer and I knelt down and pushed on his shoulders. That helped a little.

"More," David gasped, letting out as much breath as he could, hoping to make himself smaller.

"I should have gone first," I said. "I'm smaller than you are. I could have helped pull you through, and Mrs. Hemmer could have pushed."

David succeeded in getting up to his chest. Then, he raised his arms above his head. "If I can make it just a few more inches," he said as he continued to squirm. "I'm . . . almost . . . through."

He was almost through, all right . . . but, at that very moment, we heard footsteps in the hall.

They were getting louder . . . and fast.

*One of the robbers was coming!*

# 33

*"Someone's coming!"* Mrs. Hemmer hissed. *"Quick! Let's pull him back in!"*

We grabbed David's arms and pulled.

The footsteps grew louder.

We pulled harder.

The footsteps slowed. The robber was nearing, and David was still stuck.

Then . . . a voice.

"What in the world are you doing?!?!"

*Amber Caplin!*

Boy, I have never been happier to hear her voice. Sure, she's a pest, but I was glad that it was her, and not a robber!

We couldn't see her, of course, because she was in the hall. But we could talk to her.

"Amber!" I exclaimed. "Grab David's legs and pull! We're locked in the office, and this is the only way out!"

Amber did what I asked, and within seconds, David was being pulled the rest of the way through the vent. Then his face appeared through the opening.

"Come on, Rachel!" he said. "Someone could come at any minute!"

I swung my legs around and poked them through the opening. Instantly, Amber and David grabbed my feet and pulled. It was a lot easier for me to get through than it was for David! I slipped through easily, and leapt to my feet in the hall.

Through the open vent, Mrs. Hemmer's face appeared. "Hurry!" she said. "Remember what I told you! And be careful!"

I looked down the hallway in each direction, expecting to see Mr. Lakley or one of the other robbers coming. After all, we'd had some close calls, and it might be only a matter of time before we ran into them again.

*Unless they're already gone,* I thought. *They might get away, but at least we'll all be safe.*

And besides . . . I knew they wouldn't get away with it. Bad guys always get caught.

We turned left and headed toward the end of the hall, to the double doors. From there, we'd take the stairs down to the basement and find the service door that Mrs. Hemmer told us about. We hadn't seen the door the first time, but there were a lot of wax sculptures. We could easily have missed it.

"Where are we going?" Amber asked as we ran.

"To the basement!" I answered.

"Where those icky things are?!?!" she replied.

"There's a door down there!" I said. "Mrs. Hemmer said we can get outside and go for help!"

David reached the double doors and pushed them open. We sprinted through, then bolted down the stairs two at a time. Our footsteps echoed off the walls and ceiling, and we sounded like a stampede of elephants. As we rounded the landing to the next flight I tripped, but I caught myself before I fell.

Finally, we made it to the lower level, and we wasted no time racing to the door that led into the basement. David grabbed the handle and pulled the door open.

Inside the storage room, we were surprised to see not only the unfinished sculptures, but other sculptures, as well. I recognized President Eisenhower, magician Harry Houdini, and Frankenstein!

"Hey," Amber said. "Those weren't here before."

Suddenly, I realized what was going on.

"The thieves are stealing the wax figures by bringing them down here!" I exclaimed. "They're using the hidden door in the floor of the presidential room, bringing the sculptures down here, and loading them into their truck!"

David spoke. "That means they must be—"

And that's when a door suddenly burst open, and light from outside poured in. We could hear the sound of a large truck running . . . and then we heard the voice of Mr. Lakley.

*"Let's get these last three and get out of here!"* he ordered.

Oh, no! We'd gone right to the very spot where the robbers would find us!

# 34

David suddenly ducked down behind one of the unfinished wax sculptures. I did the same, and Amber followed.

*I am getting really tired of this,* I thought. *This whole day hasn't gone anything like it was planned. In fact, this isn't a field trip . . . it's a nightmare!*

From where I was hiding, I couldn't see what was going on . . . but I could hear a couple of men grunting and making noise, and I knew they were hauling the wax sculptures to the waiting truck. They would be gone soon, and we'd be able to get help.

Which kind of made me mad. I've always been taught that it's wrong to steal . . . but these men didn't seem to care. They were breaking the law, and it wasn't fair to everyone who'd worked hard to create the wax figures, and it wasn't fair to the people who worked hard to build the museum.

And that's when I saw something that gave me hope.

On the floor, next to the big vat of resin, was Mrs. Hemmer's cellular telephone! After all, she'd said she lost it somewhere in the museum! It was on the other side of the room, about ten steps away.

*If I could only reach the phone without the thieves seeing me,* I thought. *Maybe, I could call the police! I know Mrs. Hemmer said she had a hard time using her phone, because the signal kept cutting in and out . . . but it was worth a shot! If I could make it work and call the police, maybe they could get here before the robbers left!*

It was risky, but it was worth a try. Right now, the men were busy carrying the sculpture of Frankenstein out the door. I couldn't be sure, but it looked like there were only two other men besides Mr. Lakley.

I waited until they were out of the building, then I sprang. I took huge leaps. After all, it might be only a matter of seconds before the men returned to get the last sculpture.

*Six steps . . .*
*Seven . . .*
*Eight . . . .*

Then I was on top of the phone. I reached down and snapped it up, spun, and raced back to my hiding place behind one of the unfinished wax sculptures . . . just as the men came back into the room!

I couldn't believe my luck. If I had been just one second slower, I would have been in full view. Then the robbers would have spotted me, and I would have *really* been in trouble.

But just as I was thinking that I had outwitted the thieves, something happened that completely blew my cover.

*The cellular phone began ringing in my hands!*

# 35

I was in a lot of trouble, and I knew it. The thieves heard the phone, and I heard them talking.

"What's that?" one of them asked.

"It's a phone," the other man said. "It's coming from over there."

I was about to be discovered. But if that was going to happen, I was going to make sure that the robbers were discovered, too.

Quickly, I flipped open the phone, automatically turning it on. It stopped ringing . . . but I didn't speak. Instead, I placed it on the floor near one of the unfinished wax sculptures.

Knowing that the robbers were about to find me, I jumped up and leapt from my hiding place. I actually surprised the thieves, and they jumped!

"You again!" one of the men hissed. "Hey, Bill! It's one of those kids!"

Mr. Lakley appeared in the doorway.

"You guys are stealing sculptures from the wax museum!" I said. I was scared, but I was also mad. And I also knew that I had to speak loud.

"Yeah," one of the men said, "and it's a little late for you to do anything about it!"

"You and your friends have caused enough trouble," Mr. Lakley said. "I thought I'd taken care of you earlier."

"You'll never get away with it," I said. "You might have locked our whole class in the theater, and Mrs. Hemmer in your office, but the police will be here soon!"

All three of the men laughed.

"That's a good one!" one of the men said. "We're too smart for the police."

"I know what you're doing," I said. "You're stealing the wax sculptures so you can sell them for a lot of money."

"Big deal!" Mr. Lakley said. "It doesn't matter if you know what we're doing, because we're going to lock you in the museum. We've cut all the phone lines, so you can't call anyone."

"Well, someone is going to come to the wax museum to help us," I said. I spoke really loud, too.

"Come on, guys," Mr. Lakley said. "We're wasting our time. Let's get this last sculpture loaded up." Then, he looked at me. "And you," he hissed, "are going to stay right here. I'm locking the door when we leave. It'll be a long time before anyone finds any of you. By then, we'll be long gone."

"But why?" I asked. "Why are you doing this?"

"Because we want to, that's why," one of the men snapped. "And none of you kids are going to stop us."

Out of the corner of my eye, I could see David and Amber. They were still hiding, of course, and I hoped that they would stay there. But I knew they were wondering what I was doing!

The three men carefully lifted the sculpture of Harry Houdini. It was heavy, and it took a lot of effort to move it across the floor.

Then, they stopped.

At first, I didn't know why . . . and then I heard it.
*A siren!*

A siren was quickly getting louder and louder!

The men became panicky, and one of them banged into something.

*"It's the police!"* Mr. Lakley hissed. *"We've got to get out of here!"*

"But what about this statue?!?!" one of the robbers said. The sculpture of Harry Houdini was near the door, where the men had set it down.

"We don't have time!" Mr. Lakley replied. He sounded tense and anxious. "Let's get out of here while we still can!"

"It's too late!" one of the men shrieked from beyond the door. We heard the squealing of tires as they screeched to a halt, and I knew that the police had arrived.

"They're blocking the alley!" the other man shouted. "We can't get our truck out!"

"We've got to get out of here!" Mr. Lakley said. "Upstairs! Hurry!"

Mr. Lakley ran toward me, and I leapt out of his way. There was no way I was going to try to stop him!

However, as fate would have it, I didn't have to stop him. Mr. Lakley was in such a hurry that he bumped into one of the unfinished wax sculptures, lost his balance . . . and fell! He had been carrying his keys, and they jangled to the floor.

But that wasn't the best part.

The best part was, when he fell, he landed right in the—

# 36

*—vat of resin!*

There was a slurping, splooshing sound, and Mr. Lakley went completely under!

The other two men ran past me and burst up the short set of steps and through the door and through the museum, hoping to run away from the police.

David and Amber emerged from their hiding places.

"Man!" David exclaimed. "I can't believe this is happening! I just can't believe it!"

In the vat of resin, Mr. Lakley was struggling to get out. He'd grabbed the chains dangling from above, but he was having a hard time. There was so much resin on him that he must have weighed a ton! His glasses were now coated with goo, and they looked like goggles.

Finally, he succeeded in stepping out of the vat . . . but he wasn't going very far. The resin was making it impossible for him to move.

A policeman appeared in the door. "Nobody move!" he ordered.

"We're not going to," I said. Then I pointed at Mr. Lakley, all covered with resin. "And he couldn't if he wanted to!"

David and Amber laughed.

The policeman came through the door, and several others ran past in the alley. "What's going on, here?" he asked.

"That's one of the robbers!" David said, pointing at Mr. Lakley's resin-covered form. "They're stealing wax sculptures!"

"So we've heard," the policeman said. "Someone tried to call us earlier, but we were cut off. We traced the call to a cellular phone."

"That was Mrs. Hemmer's phone!" I exclaimed, kneeling down and plucking the phone from the floor. "She tried to call you, but she said she was cut off! She dropped her phone while she was trying to outrun the robbers."

"Someone at the main dispatch traced the call, and made a call back," the policeman said.

"Yes!" I said. "Just a few minutes ago! It started to ring, and I answered it . . . but I put it on the floor, hoping that whoever had called would hear what was going on!"

"That was us," the policeman said with a nod. "That's how we knew to come here. Good thinking!"

Two more uniformed policemen came in the door.

"We'll need to get this one cleaned up," one of them said, as they inspected Mr. Lakley. He was still standing next to the vat, covered with sticky goo. He didn't even look like a human being!

"But two more got away," Amber said.

"Where did they go?" asked the first policeman.

David pointed. "That way," he said, "into the museum."

"But you're safe now," the policeman said. "That's what's important."

"I'm glad this is over with," Amber said with relief.

"Me, too," David said.

In all the excitement, however, we'd forgotten one more important thing . . . .

# 37

"Our class is locked in the museum theater!" I exclaimed, stepping forward and picking up the set of keys Mr. Lakley had dropped. "And Mrs. Hemmer is locked in the office! We've got to get them out!"

"Not by yourselves," the policeman said.

Just then, two more officers rushed in through the service door. He looked at them, then pointed to us. "Go with these kids!" he instructed. "They say their entire class is locked inside the museum theater!"

The two policemen nodded for us to follow them, and we let them pass. Then, we followed them up the steps, out the door, up more stairs, through the glass double doors, and into the hallway.

173

"Mrs. Hemmer is locked in the main office," I said, fumbling with the keys in my hand. I had no idea which one would unlock the door.

"Just try them all until one works," David said.

That's what I did. We walked to the door, and I tried each key. The fifth key did the trick, and the lock turned. I pulled the door open, and was greeted by Mrs. Hemmer. She was, of course, still dressed like a she-vampire, which raised the eyebrows of the policemen.

"Don't worry," I said. "She's not really a vampire." I was sure that the policeman would want to know more . . . but right now, we had to get our class out of the theater!

"This way!" David said to the policemen. The six of us ran down the hall . . . and nearly ran into the two robbers, who were emerging from one of the rooms!

We needn't have worried, though. They had already been captured, and were wearing handcuffs. They didn't look happy at all. Two policemen were escorting them away.

We kept running until we reached the theater at the far end of the hallway. Once again, I had no idea which key would work . . . but, as luck would have it, the first key I tried was the right one! I pulled it from the lock and opened the door, then stepped inside. David,

Amber, Mrs. Hemmer, and the two policemen followed us.

On the screen, the film was just ending, and music was playing as the end credits rolled. Our classmates were still in their seats. Mrs. Tupper, however, had turned around . . . and did she ever look surprised! She must have heard us as we entered. She stood and hurried up the aisle toward us.

"David! Amber! Rachel! What is going on?!?! Why are the police here?!?! What happened?!?!"

It took a few minutes, but we explained everything. We told her all about the robbers, about how Mr. Lakley had been a crook, and how we'd been all around the museum, trying to stay away from the thieves.

"I had no idea we were locked in here," Mrs. Tupper said. "I'm glad, in a way. Otherwise, all of the students would have been worried."

"They'd be freaked, all right," David said.

"I'm just glad I don't have to hang around with you guys any more," Amber spat. "You just get me into trouble."

That was fine with me. I didn't like Amber much before today . . . and now I liked her even less.

175

Because we left the museum earlier than we'd planned, Mrs. Tupper said that we'd have to wait for another day to go out for pizza.

"Besides," she told us, "your parents might have already heard about what's happened at the wax museum. We don't want them to worry."

As we rode the bus home, David and I talked about what had happened during our field trip to the museum. It seemed so crazy. I couldn't wait to tell my mom and dad! They weren't going to believe it! But it was on the evening news, and we watched it together. They didn't say anything about David, Amber, or me, and they only briefly mentioned our class. The news story focused on the three robbers, including the director of the museum, and their plan to heist the wax sculptures and sell them to collectors in another country.

In school on Monday, however, we were heroes! Everyone knew about what had happened, and how David, Amber, and I had been partially responsible in the capture of the robbers. Everyone asked us questions and wanted to know more. It was kind of fun being so popular . . . at least for a little while.

But our popularity faded, and things got back to normal. The wax museum opened on schedule. Mrs. Hemmer was hired as the new director, and she sent

David, Amber, and me nice letters of thank you, and a free pass for each of us if we'd like to tour the museum again. I planned to go again, and soon. It would be fun . . . as long as I didn't have to hide from any more robbers!

But it wasn't to be. My dad got a notice from his company that they were transferring him to Fargo, North Dakota, which was a million miles away.

Okay, maybe not a *million* miles, but it seemed like it. It was a long way from Seattle, and Dad said that we were going to move there.

At first, I was really bummed, because I missed my friends. Fargo is a lot different than Seattle, and I was told that it was a lot colder in the winter.

But it wasn't so bad. I made new friends quickly, and I really liked my new school.

However, there was a kid who moved to our block at about the same time we did. He was really quiet, and he didn't talk much. I always said hello to him, but he only waved and walked away.

One day, he was sitting on the curb in front of his house. I walked to where he was and sat down next to him.

"You don't say much, do you?" I asked.

He shook his head, saying nothing.

"I'm Rachel," I said. "What's your name?"

"Damon Richards," he replied. That was all he said.

Still, I persisted. I asked him where he was from, and if he had any other friends. He said he was from Bismarck, which is North Dakota's state capitol. He moved here with his mom and older sister.

"You seem really shy," I said.

"Not really," he said. "I'm still trying to sort a few things out."

"Like what?" I asked. I hoped he didn't think I was prying.

"Oh, nothing you'd understand," Damon said.

"How do you know if you won't tell me what it is?" I asked.

"Oh, I'll tell you if you want," Damon replied. "But don't tell anyone else. No one will believe me. They'll all just think I'm weird."

"I won't think you're weird," I said.

"You will when I tell you about the night dragons," he said.

"The *what?!?!*" I exclaimed.

"The night dragons," he repeated.

"I promise not to think you're weird," I said, crossing my heart.

"All right," Damon said. "It all started at the beginning of summer, in Bismarck . . . ."

# Next:

# #19: North Dakota Night Dragons

Continue on for a FREE preview!

# 1

Bismarck, North Dakota is known for several things. First of all, you probably already know that Bismarck is the state capitol. You might even know that Bismarck is the home of the Dakota Zoo, which is a lot of fun. Bismarck is North Dakota's $2^{nd}$ largest city, named after German chancellor Otto von Bismarck.

Bismarck, however, is now known for something else:

Night dragons.

That's right . . . night dragons. Oh, some people don't believe they're real, just because they haven't seen them.

But if you ever do come to Bismarck, and you do go out at night, be warned:

Night dragons are real.

They are as real as anything else . . . and just because some people haven't seen them doesn't mean they're not there.

My name is Damon Richards, and I live on North 23rd Street in Bismarck. I've lived here only for a couple of years, because my dad gets transferred a lot, and we have to move. We've lived in a lot of cool places, but I really like Bismarck. I've made a lot of good friends.

The first time I saw a night dragon, I didn't think it was real. I thought I was dreaming. After all, if you saw a giant, winged creature slipping through the night sky, you'd probably think you were dreaming, too.

Now, however, I know better.

I remember that night very well. My friends and I had been outside playing a game called 'Kick the Can'. It's kind of a hide-and-seek game, and we play it a lot in the summer, right around dark.

Well, we'd just finished our game, and everyone had gone home. The sun had set and it was dark.

I was on my way home. The place where we play is at the end of our street, so I was only a few blocks from where I live. At the end of our street is Lions Hillside Skate Park, which is a lot of fun. On the other side of the skate park, however, is St. Mary's cemetery. At night, it looks pretty spooky.

Streetlights lit up the pavement and the yards. I could see lights glowing in houses as I walked. Windows were open. I could hear a few television sets, their broken fragments of sound drifting through the warm evening. Crickets chimed. The air was damp and heavy, with the thick odor of recently mowed grass.

That's when I heard it.

A noise from above.

Oh, it wasn't a plane, that's for sure. And it didn't sound like a bat or a bird.

It was a whooshing sound: slow, and heavy, deliberate, like—

Wings.

I stopped and stared into the night sky. With all of the streetlights glowing like they were, it was hard to see. The lights created a glare that clouded my vision.

Then I heard it again.

A heavy, whooshing sound, like air being pushed. I stared up into the sky, searching for whatever it was. After all, I was certain that the sound had come from above.

But I didn't hear anything more, and I didn't see anything out of the ordinary. Beneath a streetlight, a bat flitted and dove in silence, chasing a bug.

I was just about to start walking again . . . when I *did* see something.

Something in the sky.

Something *big*.

All I could see was its silhouette, a dark shadow. It swooped directly over me, turned, and sailed over a house.

And I couldn't be certain, but it looked like—

It landed. Whatever it was, it landed in the back yard, behind the Kurtzner's house. Mr. and Mrs. Kurtzner are really nice. They are like my grandparents. Sometimes, Mrs. Kurtzner makes lemonade for all of us kids on hot, summer days.

I looked behind me. The street was empty.

I looked all around. In a few homes, lights clicked off. People were settling in for the night. If I wasn't home in a few minutes, I would hear my mom calling out for me to come home.

But I've still got a few minutes, I thought, looking into the yard where I'd watched the dark shadow go. I could go and see what that thing was.

And so, I turned and walked across the lawn. I knew the Kurtzner's wouldn't mind if I went into their back yard after dark. After all . . . I wasn't doing anything wrong. I just wanted to see what had landed in their yard.

Oh, I'd find out, all right . . . but I was just moments from being scared out of my mind!

# 2

As I approached the side of the house, darkness grew. Here, the streetlights faded. I looked up, and I could see stars sprinkling across a black canopy. Several bushes grew tightly against the Kurtzner's house, and there were a few hidden crickets chirping within.

I stopped where the back yard began and gazed into the murky darkness. I could see the shadow of a large oak tree, and I could make out the faint form of a picnic table. However, I couldn't see anything else. It was just too dark.

*Maybe if I get a little closer,* I thought.

I have to admit, I was a little nervous. I wasn't sure what had made the strange whooshing sound. I wasn't sure what I'd seen. Yet, I was positive that, whatever it was, it had landed somewhere in the yard. In the tree, perhaps.

I took a step. The grass was squishy and soft beneath my feet. Somewhere, a dog barked. In the distance, a car horn honked.

I took another step. Then another, and another. Soon I was standing beneath the enormous tree. Here, beneath the limbs thick with leaves, it was darkest of all. I looked up, but I couldn't see a thing.

*This is silly,* I thought. *I must be imagining things.*

I turned to walk home. It was only a matter of minutes before Mom called for me, anyway. I looked forward to going to bed and reading my book. I was reading this really crazy story about fog phantoms in Florida. It wasn't true, but it was pretty freaky.

That's when I heard the noise. It was close by, but in the darkness, I couldn't tell where it came from. It was just a thin shuffling sound.

I looked up into the dark limbs. Even though my eyes had adjusted to the low light, I still couldn't make anything out. All I could see was darkness.

I listened . . . .

Nothing.

*This is silly,* I thought. I was just about to walk away—

Suddenly, a long claw came from around the tree. Oh, I couldn't *see* it . . . but I sure could *feel* it! Sharp talons latched onto my shoulder, and I knew right then that I'd made a big mistake by going into the Kurtzner's back yard.

You're probably thinking that I screamed.

Wrong.

I howled. I didn't know what had hold of me, but I howled as loud and as long as I could . . . which didn't last, because the creature pushed me to the ground and tackled me!

"Wait a minute! Wait a minute!" I heard a girl's voice say. I stopped struggling as she drew away. "Who are you?"

"I could ask you the same thing!" I said, trying to catch my breath. My heart was clanging in my chest, and I was gasping. The scare had really shaken me.

"No, who are you?" she repeated. "You're not Jason!"

"No, I'm not," I said. "I'm Damon Richards. Who are you?"

The girl stood, but it was still too dark to see anything but her shadowy figure. I, too, got to my feet, thankful that it had been a girl . . . and not some weird creature.

"I'm Kamryn Kurtzner," she replied. "I thought you were my cousin, Jason."

"No," I said. "I live a few houses down."

"I'm really sorry," the girl said. "I thought you were my cousin, and I was trying to scare him. He's always trying to scare me like that, and I was just trying to get him back. Man . . . you really yelled loud. Are you okay?"

"Yeah," I said. Then I laughed. "But you sure scared me. For a minute, anyway."

"What are you doing in my grandparents' back yard?" she asked.

"I . . . um . . . I thought I saw something," I replied.

"Like, what?" Kamryn asked.

"I don't know," I said, gazing up into the star-filled sky. "I . . . I thought I saw something flying. Something big."

"You saw it, too?!?!" Kamryn asked. "I was standing on the back porch, looking for Jason, when I saw something swoop through the sky. It was too dark to see what it was. It was big, though. That's why I came out into the yard. I wanted to see what it was . . . and to scare my cousin."

"I thought I saw it land here in the yard," I said. "I was on my way home, when—"

Suddenly, my mom's voice echoed from far down the street. "Daaaaamon?!?!" she called out.

I cupped my hands around my mouth. "On my way, Mom!" I shouted. Then, I turned to Kamryn. I still couldn't see her in the darkness, and I had no idea what she looked like.

"I've got to go," I said. "Maybe I'll see you around."

"I'll be here for two weeks," Kamryn replied. "I'm from Michigan, but I'm staying with my grandparents. My cousin, Jason, is here, too."

"Have a good night," I said, and I turned.

"Sorry I scared you," Kamryn said again.

"No problem," I replied. I walked away, shaking my head.

*Scared by a girl,* I thought. *Sheesh.*

Of course, I had no way of knowing that I had something else in Bismarck to worry about.

Something that would scare me far worse than I'd already been.

Something that wasn't a girl.

Something that wasn't even human.

Something that was lurking in the dark shadows at that very moment, watching me . . . and waiting.

I walked across the Kurtzner's yard and onto the sidewalk, comforted by the glowing streetlights. I've never really been afraid of the dark, but, for some reason, I was glad I was on my way home. I was glad the claws that had grabbed me hadn't been claws at all . . . only Kamryn's hands.

*But what could it have been?* I wondered. I was certain that I'd seen *something* fly over me. Something big. And I was sure it had flown over the Kurtzner's back yard. Maybe it hadn't landed, like I'd thought. I was sure I had saw *something,* though.

But, then again, maybe not. After all, it *was* very dark. With the streetlights on, it was difficult to see because of the glare. Maybe I hadn't seen anything at all.

*But Kamryn had. She said she'd seen something, and she went into the back yard to see what it was.*

What had she seen?

*Probably nothing,* I thought.

Up ahead, I could see our porch light glowing. Mom left it on until I got home.

Suddenly, I noticed something.

I stopped walking.

My skin felt tingly all over, and I had a very strange feeling . . . like I was being watched.

I looked behind me, but there was nothing to see except houses, yards, and the ribbon of sidewalk as it snaked along the street. I heard a dog bark again, a long ways off.

Then I heard the sound again. That heavy, deep *whooshing* sound, like wings.

Only this time, it was louder.

Closer.

Above me, not far above the streetlights.

I could almost see the dark shadow of something in the sky, circling.

Something *big*.

*Wa-whoosh* . . .

Something *huge* . . . .

*Wa-whoosh* . . . .

All of a sudden, an enormous dark figure dipped down, and swooped beneath the streetlight. It was so big that it blocked out the light, and a shadow fell over me.

The fact that it was so big was frightening enough . . . but when I saw what it was, I knew that my world was never going to be the same again . . . .

# 5

The creature was like nothing I'd ever seen before in my life.

Well, maybe not. I had seen creatures like this before, but they were in movies and comics and on the covers of books.

And yet, what I was seeing wasn't the cover of a book or a comic. It was straight out of the movies.

*It was a dragon!* It seemed impossible, but that's what it was!

He was deep, dark blue, with a long tail. His hind legs stretched out behind as he flew. His front claws were held forward, and it looked like he was holding on to something.

And his *wings!*

They were gigantic! The creature itself was as big as a car, but its massive wings were even bigger and wider. They thumped the air as the beast passed overhead.

And his head darted from side to side, mouth open, tongue swirling. I saw rows of long, sharp teeth. His huge, glassy eyes looked fierce and menacing as he glanced from side to side and all around. I don't think he saw me, even though I was standing right below him.

*A dragon?* I thought. *They aren't real! Dragons are only make-believe, from stories and movies!*

Yet—

I was sure of what I'd seen. There was no way I could mistake it for an owl or anything else. It was just too big.

The dragon turned his head, like he was looking for something. He turned and circled beneath the light.

Suddenly, in the distance, I heard a throaty cry. It sounded angry. The dragon turned his head, and spewed a plume of fire from his mouth!

*This isn't real,* I thought. *I'm going to wake up any moment now, I just know it.*

But I didn't. I wasn't dreaming. I wasn't imagining. What was going on was *real*. There really *was* a dragon, circling in the sky above me.

Then, I heard another loud, animal-like shriek. It was as loud as a trumpet! Whatever it was, it was close . . . and getting closer by the second!

And when I saw what was making the sound, my knees turned to rubber. I sank to the grass, too terrified to even stand. All I could do was kneel and look up, my mouth open in disbelief.

*Above me, in the sky, a horrifying black dragon was attacking the blue one!*

# FUN FACTS ABOUT WASHINGTON:

State Capitol: Olympia

State Fossil: Columbian Mammoth

State Nickname: The Evergreen State

State Gem: Petrified Wood

State Bird: Willow Goldfinch

State Fish: Steelhead Trout

State Tree: Western Hemlock

State Insect: Green Darner Dragonfly

State Flower: Pink Rhodendron

Statehood: November 11th, 1889 (42nd state)

# FAMOUS WASHINGTONIANS!

**Bing Crosby, singer and actor**

**Bill Gates, software developer**

**Jimi Hendrix, guitarist**

**Francis Scobee, astronaut**

**Hank Ketcham, cartoonist**

**Judy Collins, singer**

**Bob Barker, TV host**

**Chester F. Carlson, inventor**

**Smohalla, Indian prophet and chief**

**among many, many more!**

# ABOUT THE AUTHOR

Johnathan Rand is the author of more than 50 books, with well over 2 million copies in print. Series include **AMERICAN CHILLERS, MICHIGAN CHILLERS, FREDDIE FERNORTNER, FEARLESS FIRST GRADER**, and **THE ADVENTURE CLUB.** He's also co-authored a novel for teens (with Christopher Knight) entitled **PANDEMIA**. When not traveling, Rand lives in northern Michigan with his wife and two dogs. He is also the only author in the world to have a store that sells only his works: **CHILLERMANIA!** is located in Indian River, Michigan. Johnathan Rand is not always at the store, but he has been known to drop by frequently. Find out more at:

**www.americanchillers.com**